"WHO WAS THAT MASKED MAN, ANYWAY?"

"A RICHARD JACKSON BOOK"

"WHO WAS THAT MASKED MAN, ANYWAY?"

"by AVI"

Orchard Books   New York

The author expresses thanks to the following for permission to quote excerpts from historic radio broadcasts. CAPTAIN MIDNIGHT, "The First Show in the Series," September 30, 1940. Copyright © 1971, The Radiola Co. Used with permission. THE SHADOW character, copyrights, and trademarks are owned by The Condé Nast Publications. THE LONE RANGER, "Bud Titus Resigns." Courtesy of Palladium Limited Partnership. SKY KING, "The Land of the Diamond Scarab," as heard on ABC radio on July 14, 1947. Copyright © 1987, The Radiola Co. Used with permission. THE GREEN HORNET, "The Woman in the Case." Copyright © 1944, Charles Michelson, Inc. Used with permission. Excerpt from BUCK ROGERS, April 4, 1939. Copyright © 1971, The Radiola Co. Used with permission.

Permission to quote from the following textbook is gratefully acknowledged. ON THE LONG ROAD. Copyright © 1940, renewed, Silver Burdett Company. Used with permission.

Orchard Books, 95 Madison Avenue, New York, NY 10016

Manufactured in the United States of America
Book design by Mina Greenstein
The text of this book is set in 12 point Caledonia and
10 point Clarinda Typewriter.
2   4   6   8   10   9   7   5   3   1

Library of Congress Cataloging-in-Publication Data
Avi, date.
Who was that masked man, anyway? / by Avi.
p.   cm. "A Richard Jackson book."
Summary: In the mid-forties when nearly everyone else is
thinking about World War II, sixth-grader Frankie Wattleson
gets in trouble at home and at school because of his
preoccupation with his favorite radio programs.
ISBN 0-531-05457-8.   ISBN 0-531-08607-0 (lib. bdg.)
[1. Radio serials—Fiction.   2. World War, 1939–1945—
United States—Fiction.   3. Teacher-student relationships—
Fiction.   4. Imagination—Fiction.]   I. Title.
PZ7.A953Wk   1992   [Fic]—dc20   92-7942

"For Gabriel"

"Episode 1"

"And now . . .

"Ovaltine—that superdelicious drink that builds bright minds and strong bodies eight ways—presents . . .

" 'The Radio Adventure Hour'!

"You are about to hear a series of strange, exciting, and perilous adventures that will lead us to all parts of the world.

"But first, we take you to France. The war has reached a moment of crisis. The Allied army is close to terrible destruction.

"In a small, bombproof dugout the light of a candle flame flickers across the strained face of a general of the Allied army. Outside, the night is dark and cold. Suddenly, we hear—"

"Major Steel?"

"Sir, everything is prepared."
"You've found the man?"
"I have."
"What's his name? No! It's better that I
don't know."
"I agree with you, sir."
"There are only two people in the world who
know the mission to which he has been assigned.
You and our leader in Washington."
"Yes, sir."
"Major, do you think he has a chance?"
"I'm afraid the odds against him are about
one hundred to one."
"If he fails, it will be terrible for us all.
It will— But enough of that. Bring him in."
"Yes, sir."
"Wait! I don't want to see his face. Blow out
the candle."
"Yes, sir."
"Now bring him in."
"Yes, sir. Will you come in, Captain? The man
is before you, sir."
"You have your instructions?"
"Yes, sir."
"Then I want you to be sure you understand
the risks you are facing."
"I do."
"If you fail tonight, it will be the end for
all of us. If you are successful, our country
will be saved from defeat. Do you understand?"
"I do."
"Also, if you succeed tonight, you will have

started a long and perilous task that, if you live, may require your lifetime to complete. Is that clear?"

"Yes, General. Very clear."

"Above all, you understand that the ultimate purpose is the extermination of the most rascally and menacing criminal in the world! A traitor to the United States! A fiend who has cost the lives of thousands of your countrymen! I am speaking of the one known as . . . Ivan Carr."

"I understand."

"You are ready to go?"

"My plane stands outside the door."

"Good. How long do you think it will be before we know the outcome of this night's venture?"

"Sir, if I've not returned by midnight, you will know I've failed."

"You are a brave man, Captain. Now, Godspeed."

"Thank you, sir."

"And so, into the night roars a plane piloted by a lone man upon whose shoulders rests the fate of his country.

'Hours later—"

"AW, MA! Turn the radio back on! The show's almost over!"

"Frankie, you're supposed to be doing homework, not listening to garbage!"

"Ma, it's not garbage. It's 'Captain Midnight.' Please! Can't I just listen to the end of the program?"

"That's all you're interested in—radio. Now get up to your room. Scat! Go on!"

"I'm going."

"All this racket. . . . Your father will be home tired and upset."

"He's always tired and upset."

"Young man, in case you didn't know it, there's a *world* war going on. There's a service star in our window."

"Just means family's in the war."

"Frankie! Your brother got wounded fighting for your freedom."

"What about the freedom to listen to the radio?"

"Franklin Delano Wattleson, do you want me to *destroy* that radio?"

"No!"

"Then go up to your room *immediately* and do your homework for once!"

"Do you know when Tom's coming home?"

"When he's well enough. Now, go!"

"I'm going."

"And be quiet. Mr. Swerdlow is studying."

"He went out."

"I don't care where he went."

"HEY, MARIO! *Psst!* Mario! Open your window! I have to talk to you."

"I'm doing my homework."

"You're always doing your homework."

"Yeah, well, we're supposed to."

"Oh, boy, you're so lucky to have a radio in your room. Wish I could."

"What do you want?"

"Did you hear 'Captain Midnight'? It was about how he began."

"I was doing my long divisions."

"That mean you finished your math?"

"Sure."

"I was going to. But 'Sky King' came on and he was being chased by giants. Then 'Captain Midnight.' It was so great I forgot about my math."

"Frankie, I gotta go. My mother wants me to have my schoolwork done by the time she gets home."

"Mario! Wait!"

"What?"

"What about geography? You get the principal products of Australia?"

"Yeah."

"Hand them over."

"You know, one of these days when I pass my homework to you, it's going to drop between the buildings."

"I'd go down and get it."

"What if it were night and it was dark?"

"Streetlamp shines through."

"Or your glasses broke."

"I'd feel my way."

"Anyway, how come I'm the one that always does the homework?"

"'Cause you're the one that gets the A's."

"So?"

"I don't get them in anything."

"Miss Gomez says you're a daydreamer. And Billy says you're setting a world record for being kept in after school. Thirty-eight times."

"None of his beeswax."

"Miss Gomez knows you copy my work."

"How come?"

"She asked me."

"Gee whillikers, you *told*?"

"Well, she wanted to know why we always have the same answers. So I said we live in these houses with rooms and windows opposite, so we work together. Then I said your father works two jobs. That your brother got wounded in the Pacific and will be home soon. That your mother takes in a boarder whose name is Mr. Swerdlow, who's studying to be a doctor."

"Why'd you tell her all that?"

"She asked me."

"Nosey Parker. . . . Hey, Mario!"

"What?"

"You like the way Miss Gomez looks?"

"Hubba-hubba."

"She could have been a movie star. Good as Veronica Lake. But—guess what?"

"What?"

"I saw her cry."

"Veronica Lake?"

"No. Miss Gomez."

"When?"

"Last week."

"What happened?"

"Her boyfriend got wounded in Europe."

"Oh. My mother says anyone who fights in the war is a hero."

"Your father was."

"I told you, Frankie . . . I don't like talking about him."

"Sorry. . . . Hey, you know what? Miss Gomez's boyfriend's name is Mitch."

"How'd you find out?"

"Four Wheaties box tops plus two bits."

"What's that got to do with it?"

"I got the *Jack Armstrong Detective Instruction Booklet.* So last time when Miss Gomez kept me in after school, I saw a letter on her desk."

"And you *looked?*"

"Sure. When she went out of the room, I read it."

"That's snooping."

"No, it's not, dumbbell. It's what the booklet says to do."

"You know how bad your brother got wounded yet?"

"Just that he was on this secret mission. Got parachuted down into the Japanese High Command airport."

"That true?"

"Told you, it's a secret. But I know what his general said to him."

"What?"

"Said, 'You are a brave man, Tom.' "

"He'll get a Purple Heart for being wounded."

"Your dad got one, didn't he?"

"Yeah. . . ."

"Wish I could see it."

"My mother keeps it with her. Hey, Frankie."

"What?"

"Maybe with Miss Gomez's boyfriend being wounded, he'll be so different she won't like him anymore and she'll want a *new* boyfriend."

"She could get one, easy."

"Maybe your brother."

"Naw. Tom'd rather be a hero. Or a spy. Or a cowboy. They can like girls. Just can't marry 'em."

"Why?"

"Too busy. Wait a minute!"

"What?"

" 'The Shadow' is coming on!"

"Frankie—"

"Hurry! Turn it on loud."

''Who knows what evil lurks in the hearts of men?''

"The Shadow knows! Ha—ha—ha—ha—ha!"

"Your neighborhood Blue Coal dealer brings you the thrilling adventures of the Shadow, the hard and relentless fight of one man against the forces of evil. These dramatizations are designed to demonstrate forcefully to old and young alike that crime does not pay.

"Government forecasts indicate that homeowners may face another shortage of all types of fuel for home heating. You're fortunate if you heat with coal because you're able to store fuel. Call your Blue Coal dealer tomorrow and place your order so he can schedule early delivery. Make sure that you order the right size for your furnace. And, if you are not sure what it should be, ask your Blue Coal dealer. He'll be glad to inspect your heating plant and may be able to make other recommendations too that will help you get more heat and burn less fuel. Tomorrow, first thing, call the nearest Blue Coal dealer. And ask him to schedule your supply of blue coal for early delivery.

"The Shadow, who aids the forces of law and order, is in reality Lamont Cranston, wealthy young man—about—town. Years ago, in the Orient, Cranston learned a strange and mysterious secret, the hypnotic power to cloud men's minds so they cannot see him. Cranston's friend and companion, the lovely Margo Lane, is the only person who knows to whom the voice of the invisible Shadow belongs.

"Today's drama: Curse of the Gypsies."

"HEY! Why'd you turn it off?"

"That makes me too nervous. My mother doesn't want me getting that way."

"Mario, you're only *listening*."

"She says doing starts with listening."

"You going to give me the math?"

"I don't know."

"If you do, I'll let you see the skeleton."

"Mr. Swerdlow's?"

"His room is empty. Tonight's his night class. You can come over now."

"Promise I'll see it?"

"Cross my heart and hope to die. I'll put the board across."

"Someday that board is going to break and one of us is going to fall."

"Captain Midnight goes out windows all the time."

"I'm not Captain Midnight."

"Here it comes. Okay. I'm set here. Your end right?"

"Yeah."

"Come on, then."

"I mean it, Frankie. It's an old board."

"See, it didn't break. If you weren't so nervous all the time—"

"Aw, cheese it."

"Ready?"

"Yeah."

"Okay. Here goes. Ta-da! Chet Barker, Master Spy!"

"Da-dum, dum-da!"

"Shredded Corn Crunch brings you another thrilling adventure of Chet Barker, Master Spy! Chet Barker, ruthless, clear-eyed, brave, and smartly dressed! Chet Barker, thundering out of the dim past in a constant search for his true identity! Chet Barker, fighting hand to hand for what's right. On the land!"

"On the sea!"

"And in the air! Ta-dum! With his faithful but brilliant sidekick, Skipper O'Malley, Chet Barker *believes* in the American way!"

"Da-dum!"

"And now for today's adventure, The Secret of the Skeleton.

"As we find our young heroes, they've just landed outside the headquarters of the German High Command, having parachuted down from a B-17 that was painted invisible. So no one saw us."

"Are *we* invisible?"

"Wouldn't be fair. Now we open the secret back door to the headquarters. It creaks. Then I say, 'Keep low, Skipper.' You say, 'I read you, Chet.' "

"I read you, Chet."

"I say, 'You have your instructions?' You say, 'I do.' "

"I do."

"If we fail tonight, it will be the end for all of us.

If we're successful, our country will be saved from defeat. Do you understand? You say, 'You bet.' "

"You bet."

"Then we crawl along the highway, making sure no one hears or sees us. I say, 'Hold it, Skipper.' You say, 'What's up?' "

"What's up?"

"Guard coming. You say, 'I'll take care of him.' "

"I'll take care of him."

"You do."

"*Bang! Blam!* I did."

"Okay. Up the steps. Hold it. Another guard. No! Great Scott! Three of them. We fight. *Sock! Pow! Wham!*"

"*Biff!*"

"Got 'em. You say, 'Phew! That was a close call, Chet.' "

"Phew! That was a close call, Chet."

" 'Tweren't nothing, Skip. Look! The main dungeon!"

"Mr. Swerdlow's door?"

"Right."

"You really sure he's not there?"

"I told you—he went to class. Come on. Say, 'I see it.' "

"I see it."

"Our two heroes crawl forward, barely daring to draw breath. Chet says, 'Made it! Wasn't sure we would.' Skipper says, 'I didn't know either.' "

"That's dumb, Frankie."

"Mario, that's what sidekicks *say*!"

"Okay. I didn't know either."

"Now, you carry me the rest of the way."

"Why?"

"I got wounded."

"When?"

"Before."

"You never said."

"I can't say everything."

"Why is it me that's always carrying you?"

"Mario, don't you know *anything* about sidekicks? That's what they *do*. Besides, you're too fat for me to carry."

"I'm not fat. I'm husky."

"Mario, do you want to see Mr. Swerdlow's skeleton or not?"

"Yeah."

"Well, just pretend you carried me."

"Okay. I just did."

"I say, 'Thanks for saving my life, pardner. I can scramble on my own now.' You say, ' 'Tweren't nothing.' "

" 'Tweren't nothing."

"I say, 'The coast is clear.' I reach up and try the trapdoor. It opens slowly. Eerie organ music. Echo of feet on stone floor. Sound of water dripping. You look around with big eyes and say, 'Mighty creepy in here, Chet.' "

"Mighty creepy in here, Chet."

"I say, 'What's the matter, Skip? Getting nervous?' "

"Frankie, can't we just go in?"

"Come on, Mario. We have to do it right! You say, 'Chet, I can't help it. I just keep thinking of my loved ones back home.' "

"You mean my mother?"

"Well, sure. You love her, don't you?"

"You making fun of my mother?"

"No, I'm just saying she's home, right?"

"Most of the time she works."

"Mario, you know what I mean! Just *say* it."

"Okay. I can't help it. I just keep thinking of my loved ones back home."

"Don't worry, Skipper. It's for a good cause. The best cause there is. The freedom of every red-blooded man, woman, and child in the free world. That's why we do it. It's not the glory."

"Or the money."

"I'm supposed to say that."

"Frankie! Just open the door!"

"Okay. Here we are. I twist the triple lock. Find the secret switch. *Click! Ping! Wocket!* Okay. I open the vault. Sound of rusty hinges. Wind. Thunder. Lightning. Rain. The music swells. I say, 'Great Scott! There it is—Dr. Swerdlow's secret skeleton!' "

"Hey, Frankie, you know what? Doctors must be strange."

"Why?"

"Look. One suit. Three shirts. Two pairs of shoes. And a skeleton. All hanging in the closet."

"Student doctors have to learn the parts."

"What do you think happened to the head?"

"Not allowed to take the skull."

"How come?"

"Skulls are always cursed. Only evil people keep skulls."

"Is Mr. Swerdlow evil?"

"Beginning to think so."

"How come?"

"Most of the time he's so quiet, you know, like his mind was clouded by something strange and mysterious."

"Frankie, who do you think—you know—*before*—who do you think the skeleton was?"

"Someone famous."

"How can you tell?"

"You wouldn't want to save just any bunch of bones, would you?"

"Hey, I just thought. . . . What if it's a . . . you know, a woman."

"Could be."

"If it is, it's the first lady I ever saw without clothes."

"Mario, it's just bones."

"Yeah, but if I told my mother she'd still get mad. She doesn't want me looking at women without clothes."

"Maybe it's a man."

"Said I wasn't to look at them either. Hey, Frankie?"

"What?"

"How come the bones are all brown?"

"Because they got it from a pyramid. See, Skipper, these bones were a king of Egypt. Touch it and it brings a curse. The Curse of the Closet Mummy! Dar'st you go into the vault and close the closet door, Skipper?"

"What about you, Chet? I double dare you!"

"I'm in, Skipper. What about you?"

"See. I'll even shut the door."

"And so we come to another end of another Chet Barker, Master Spy, adventure."

"With his faithful sidekick, Skipper."

"Tune in tomorrow for excitement."

"Thrills!"

"And adventure! Yes, radio fans, find out tomorrow what Chet Barker and his sidekick, Skipper O'Malley, discover inside the closet with the ancient skeleton when suddenly they—"

"Frankie!"

"What?"

"Listen."

"What?"

"Someone's coming in the room!"

"It's Swerdlow!"

"My mother's going to be so—"

"Shhh!"

"I hear voices in the air that have never been so—"

"What's he singing?"

"Shhh!"

"Rare. . . . What the . . . ?"

"Oh, hi, Mr. Swerdlow."

"Hello, Mr. Swerdlow."

"Frankie?"

"Yes, sir."

"Who's that with you?"

"Mario Calvino, sir."

"Oh, yes. . . . What are you boys doing in there?"

"We heard a moan and thought it might be the skeleton."

"A what?"

"A moan."

"What kind of moan?"

"Like something was dying, or worse."

"Come out of there, please!"

"Yes, sir. See, Mario never saw a skeleton before."

"I'm sure that's too bad, but—"

"I was trying to cheer him up. See, Mr. Swerdlow, Mario's father was killed in the war."

"I'm sorry to hear that, but . . . look here, boys, I need a skeleton for my studies. It is very valuable. And you might break it."

"Must be a jillion skeletons in Europe or the Pacific."

"Frankie, I told you before. Privacy is important to me. I don't want you coming in here."

"This used to be my brother's room."

"So you've said, many times. That's nothing to do with me. And I've had a rough day. I don't need to find kids lurking in my closet."

"Yes, sir."

"Frankie, the last time this happened, you promised you wouldn't do it again."

"I know, sir."

"Well, this time I intend to let your mother know."

"Oh, please, sir, she'll put me on the rack!"

"The what?"

"The rack. It's like an ancient toaster."

"Don't be absurd. Come on."

"Yes, sir."

"You too, Mario."

"Yes, sir."

"Down the steps, Frankie."

"Mr. Swerdlow? Can I ask you something as we go?"

"What?"

"How come your day was so rough?"

"I was assisting in surgery."

"Wow!"

"Very tiring."

"Were you . . . cutting up people?"

"Putting them together, actually."

"Was it anyone you knew?"

"For goodness' sake!"

"Were they soldiers?"

"Frankie, I really don't want to talk about it."

"Yes, sir. . . . Mr. Swerdlow?"

"Yes, Frankie?"

"If my brother, Tom, needs putting together, think you could do it? I mean, you could use the kitchen. I could help."

"You are the most extra—"

"Mr. Swerdlow, before you speak to my ma, can I ask you just one other thing?"

"What is it?"

"If a person found an extra arm, could you attach it to someone who already had two arms?"

"Frankie!"

"Yes, sir."

"Ah, Mrs. Wattleson. . . ."

"Why, Mr. Swerdlow. And Frankie? Mario, when did you come into the house? I didn't hear the doorbell."

"I . . ."

"I asked him over."

"Mrs. Wattleson, I'm afraid I found Frankie in my room again. This time he had his friend with him."

"Frankie, how many times have I told you . . ."

"Mrs. Wattleson, I just cannot have this. I simply can't. They were in the closet."

"Mr. Swerdlow, cross my heart, hope to die, and no fins. It won't happen again. I'll never, ever—"

"Be quiet, Frankie!"

"Mrs. Wattleson, I'm sorry to have to complain—"

"No, no, Mr. Swerdlow. You have rights. I understand. And I promise, his father will punish him so hard he'll remember for the rest of his life. And Mr. Swerdlow . . ."

"Yes?"

"I was planning to make some apple dumplings. I'll make one for you too."

"Oh, thank you. That's very nice."

"Good-night, Mr. Swerdlow."

"Good-night, Mrs. Wattleson."

"Mario . . ."

"Mrs. Wattleson, please don't tell my mother on me. She gets so upset and—"

"I'll think about it, Mario. You just get on home now."

"Yes, ma'am, I'm going. Bye, Frankie."

"Bye."

"Now, Franklin, as for you . . . what were you doing up there?"

"Ma, see, Mr. Swerdlow's got this skeleton in his closet, and the other day on 'Buck Rodgers'—"

"Young man, your father is going to hear about this. And I'll tell you another thing. I'm going to take that radio—"

"Ma!"

"Do you think money grows on trees? If Mr. Swerdlow moved out, do you think it would be just nothing to get someone respectable like that to take that room for ten dollars a week?"

"It's Tom's room."

"Your mouth is too fresh!"

"Ma . . ."

"It's all that radio! You don't know what's in your head and what's coming out of that box. One of these days they'll put you in a crazy house. But I'll tell you another thing, Mr. Adventures, this time, no radio for a *week*!"

"Ma!"

"Now get on up to your room. Fast!"

"I just want to know. . . . Were you really making apple dumplings?"

"Of course not. But Mr. Swerdlow loves them, and it'll make him forget what you did. As if I didn't have better things to do. Now get up to your room."

"HEY, MARIO! *Psst!* Mario!"

"Oh, boy. . . . You always get me in so much trouble. If my mother learns . . . You don't know. She starts crying about my father, and then her mother, then her father, then her sister, then me, then her, then all her relatives. And she's got a lot. She never stops."

"Honest, Mario, I'm sorry. But you know what?"

"What?"

"You're the first person to know: I've sworn a vow."

"About what?"

"I don't care how hard and relentless he is—I'm going to get Mr. Swerdlow."

"Why?"

"You heard: I begged him not to tell my ma or she'd put me on the rack."

"But that wasn't true."

"Yeah, but he didn't know. Anyway, he said he was operating on people."

"That's his job."

"There wasn't any blood on his hands."

"Some people wash their hands, you know."

"Except I happen to know he's supposed to be in some class, not operating."

"Maybe it was an emergency."

"It's fishy—that's all."

"Frankie, you're *always* thinking something's fishy. I'll see you in school tomorrow."

"Hey, Mario, could you leave your window open?"

"Come on, Frankie, I really have to finish my homework. Soon as my mother gets back, the first thing she'll say is, 'Did you do your reader?' Or something like that. Gets upset if it's not done."

"I hate that reader."

"Why?"

"Supposed to be a *reader*, with stories, right? But there's nothing to read but *words*. Okay, just keep your window open, right?"

"Why?"

"Time for 'Iceman.' "

"Frankie . . . my mother. . . ."

"You are a brave man, Skipper. One of the best. So just put your radio on your window ledge and play it low."

"But—"

"Skipper, if a hero can't count on his sidekick, it will be terrible for us all."

''The legend of *Iceman!*

''In the Ice Age—thousands of years ago—Thorgun was a hunter who defended his people from killer beasts. Then, trapped beneath a glacier, Thorgun remained buried for twelve thousand years while his body was pressed into the hardness of diamonds. Thawed out in the twentieth century, Thorgun found his way to Bay City, where—in the guise of Thor Benson, simple shoe salesman—he combined the keen instincts of the ancient hunter with a body as hard as a diamond, to become *Iceman!*

''With his youthful companion, Kevin Morris, at his side, Iceman defends innocent citizens from criminals whose wolflike greed will stop at nothing.

"But before today's thrilling adventure, let's hear from Sam Babbitt. Okay, Sam."

"Say, kids, last week a soldier on home leave was over at my place examining some *POW!* model soldiers I had. When he was there, he said something interesting. He remarked that those *POW!* soldiers were among the most authentic reproductions he'd ever seen and would be great for training troops in frontline observation posts. What's more, he felt you could learn a lot from them too.

"And I'm sure you *have* learned too, if you've been choosing that fantastic cereal Rogers' *POW!* for your particular breakfast meal. I hardly need to tell you that inside each box of *POW!* there's a colored cardboard cutout of a soldier all ready to assemble. You don't have to send in one penny for it. Not even a box top. And remember, there are twelve special model soldiers you can find. Six American, two British, two French, and two Russian. On each model— printed right on the back—it tells you about the soldier's rank, the kind of fighting he's trained to do, as well as the guns he carries. What's more, you'll get important tips on how to identify these Allied soldiers from a distance so you don't confuse them with enemy troops.

"So, kids, if you haven't started to collect these nifty model soldiers, you'll want to start today. Tell your mom to get you a box of those good-tasting, golden rice flakes. When you do, you'll discover a new model soldier inside.

Start putting together your own Allied army to—
day! And don't forget, the name is *POW! P-O-W-!*

"And now, Iceman!"

"Yesterday the Bay City Police discovered an
unconscious masked boy on the streets of the Mission District. At a nearby hospital they pro-
vided medical help while trying to learn the
boy's identity. But the one thing the boy would
not allow was the removal of his mask. Instead,
he kept calling for Police Commissioner Walton.
It was Nurse Donnegan who brought Commissioner
Walton to the boy's room."

"And you say, Nurse, this masked boy keeps
asking for me?"

"That's right, Commissioner."

"Hmmm."

"The doctors are convinced he's deeply troubled about something."

"Describe him for me, Nurse."

"He's no more than twelve, has sandy brown
hair, a firm jaw, and, behind his white mask, the
clearest blue eyes you could ever imagine."

"Did you say *white* mask?"

"That's right, Commissioner—white."

"Better let me have a word with him."

"Yes, sir. There you are—that's him."

"Is that you, Commissioner Walton?"

"Yes, it is."

"Thank goodness, sir. But I have to speak to
you alone."

"Nurse, you can leave now. All right, Kevin,
she's gone."

"Oh, Commissioner, you don't know how glad I
am to see you."

"Kevin, the moment they told me you were wearing the white mask, I knew it had to be you and
that it had something to do with Iceman. What's
happened?"

"Commissioner, Iceman is gone, disap-
peared!"

"What! Better tell me more."

"That's just it, Commissioner. I can't. You
know how long Iceman's lived—"

"Twelve thousand years."

"But he told me he was about to crack a case
that was the biggest hunt of his *life*, the most
serious thing that ever happened."

"Holy smokes!"

"That the fate of the entire universe depended on it—"

"Good grief!"

"But now he's vanished!"

⚡

"FRANKIE, your father's home."

"Ma, 'Iceman' is just—"

"Frankie! I told you, you're not supposed to be
listening to radio. Mario, take that radio away from
the window! Frankie, come downstairs."

" 'LO, POP."

"Frankie. Come on—sit down. Look, your ma
says you were bothering Mr. Swerdlow again."

"Not really."

"What does 'not really' mean?"

"I was just conducting an investigation."

"A what?"

"I think he may have possible criminal influences."

"Frankie, I'm only just eating my dinner. I put in my day at the plant, and then do you know where I was tonight?"

"Working."

"Right. Helping Mr. Giorgi fix toilets."

"It's not the most serious thing that ever happened."

"Frankie, let me tell you something. There is a war going on over *there*. We don't need one here. Do you understand what I'm saying, *really* understand?"

"Holy smokes!"

"What did you say?"

"I said I understand."

"Go to bed."

"Episode 2"

"FRANKIE! Time to go. Enough breakfast."

"Ma, I want to get to school alert, full of vigor and vim, so I can be a tip-top student!"

"Four bowls is enough."

"But I *love POW!*"

"You're going to be late."

"Just one more glass of Ovaltine. Did you know that's what Captain Midnight drinks?"

"Frankie, you'll be going to the bathroom all day! Now scoot!"

"Where's Pop?"

"Why do you have to know everything? He's on an early shift. Now just go."

"GOOD MORNING, Class Six-B."

"Good morning, Miss Gomez!"

"As I told you, we'll start off today with our *On the Long Road* readers. Please take them out of your desks and open to page two seventy-one. That's the chapter I asked you to read last night, so you shouldn't have any trouble. Brigid, why don't you start reading today."

"Me?"

"Yes, Brigid, you. Go on, now. Right from the top of page two seventy-one."

"Now?"

"Yes, Brigid, now."

"Page two seventy-one?"

"Yes. From the top."

"Now?"

"Go ahead, dear."

" 'One clear evening in early spring Uncle Jack called for Bob and soon they were riding up the mountain road in the automobile when they reached the top of the mountain Uncle Jack parked the car but now he and Bob walked to a rock not far from the ob . . . ob—' "

"Observatory. Brigid, you don't have to read so quickly."

"Yes, Miss Gomez. 'Observatory let's sit down here said Uncle Jack this will be a good place to begin your study of astronomy we can get a fine view of the sky from here now what are some of the questions you would like to ask me Bob looked up and—' "

"Just a moment, Brigid. Franklin Wattleson, Mario Calvino, bring your books up here, please.

No, no. With what you have inside them too. Now, what is that, Franklin?"

"A magazine."

"Tell the class what it's called."

"*Radio Digest.*"

"And you, Mario?"

"*Radio Builder.*"

"And, Mario, what are we supposed to be reading?"

"*On the Long Road.*"

"Then why are you two reading something else?"

"Well . . ."

"I know!"

"All right, Franklin. Tell the class."

"See, class, *Radio Digest* gives you the inside scoop on all your favorite radio shows. It's chockfull of tips on how they do sound effects like Silver's hoofbeats or the sound of flying. And, gang, not only will it tell you about the radio stars, but all your favorite radio writers too. So, boys and girls, if you haven't yet started your collection of this nifty magazine—"

"Class! That's enough, Franklin! Franklin and Mario, you may stand in the corner the entire reading session."

"But—"

"But what, Franklin?"

"If I put my face into the corner, it might squeeze it into a wedge. Like a piece of cheese. It'd be like being on 'Dick Tracy'! People would call me Wedge-Face!"

"Class! And for *that* remark, Franklin Wattleson, you may stay after school for an hour."

"ALL RIGHT, Franklin, sit in the middle of your seat, feet flat on the floor, back straight, with your hands clasped before you."

"Yes, Miss Gomez."

"Do you understand why I asked you to stay today?"

"I said something I shouldn't."

"Exactly. You were being cheeky, weren't you?"

"Yes, Miss Gomez."

"I think I should warn you, Franklin, you're becoming a serious problem. What would your parents say if I gave them a call?"

"You can't."

"Why?"

"We don't have a phone. We use the one at Pearlman's Candy Store."

"Well, I'm sure I could write to your parents."

"I could intercept it."

"That would be breaking the law."

"Miss Gomez, my ultimate purpose is the extermination of the most rascally and dangerous criminal in the world."

"Franklin, how would your parents like it if I informed them that you copy Mario's homework?"

"Miss Gomez, if my father knew, he would feed me to the boa constrictor he keeps in the basement."

"Franklin, you are constantly in another world. With all this imagination you could *do* so much better. Do you know how much potential you have?"

"Yup."

"During geography, what were you thinking about?"

"Things. . . ."

"What things?"

"I don't think I should say."

"I won't bite your head off."

"Well, the other night, the Green Hornet got into this terrible fix."

"Green Hornet?"

"On the radio."

"Of course."

"Usually his sidekick, Kato, is there to . . . See, the Green Hornet needs to talk to *someone*. But then Kato got shot. In the leg. He'll be all right. Just a flesh wound. But, Britt Reid—that's the Green Hornet—did you know Britt Reid was the Lone Ranger's great-grandnephew?—he was mostly talking to himself. What I was thinking is, what if people heard him? I mean, if heroes didn't have sidekicks, people would think they were, well, sort of goofy, right? That's what I was thinking about."

"All that?"

"Yeah."

"But what about the principal products of Australia, Franklin? Don't you think you need to learn that sort of thing?"

"I don't know."

"Well, I do know. And I think you need to focus on what we're learning here."

"The principal product of Australia is sheep."

"There, you *do* know."

"Miss Gomez?"

"Yes."

"I think 'The Green Hornet' is much more interesting."

"But when you grow up, Franklin, it may well be that you'll need to know about Australian products."

"I never heard a hero who talked about sheep."

"Franklin, you're not a hero. Not yet."

"But Miss Gomez, by listening to the radio I'm learning to be one. Do you want to be a teacher all the time?"

"Do you know, Franklin, though I'm willing to admit that I've never met a boy quite like you, I'm beginning to think a home visit will really be necessary. What's more—"

"Miss Gomez?"

"Oh, Mrs. Welsby. I didn't hear you come in. Franklin and I were just having some quiet time."

"Oh, I didn't realize . . . Miss Gomez, I'm . . . I'm . . . afraid this . . . this . . . telegram just came."

"Telegram?"

"It's for you. I'll be glad to stay with the boy while you . . ."

"No . . . I . . ."

"Miss Gomez . . . is it very painful? Here, sit down. Let me get you a glass of water."

"That's all right."

"Are you sure?"

"Yes."

"I'm going to get you some water. I'll be right back."

"Thank you."

"Miss Gomez?"

"Yes, Franklin."

"Do you want me to go?"

"I . . ."

"The other principal products of Australia are wool and dairy stuff."

"Yes, Franklin. You can go now."

"Miss Gomez?"

"Yes, Franklin."

"Is it . . . Mitch?"

"How did you know his name?"

"I read the *Jack Armstrong Detective Instruction Booklet*."

"Oh. . . ."

"Did Mitch . . . croak?"

"Oh, God. . . ."

"Gee. I'm sorry. Honest. Really. I am."

"HEY, MARIO! MARIO!"

"Shut your window. You always get me into so much trouble."

"Gotta tell you something important."

"What?"

"It's about Miss Gomez. What happened to her."

"What?"

"Let me get over."

"My mother'll be home soon."

"Never mind. Here's the board. Okay. Fixed here. Fixed there?"

"Yeah."

"Coming over."

"Be careful!"

"I am. Okay."

"What is it?"

"Listen. Miss Gomez kept me in class, right?"

"So what? She always does."

"And we were sitting there talking about sheep when Mrs. Welsby came in."

"The principal?"

"Right."

"Why she do that?"

"That's what I'm telling. Mrs. Welsby walks in. *Step. Step.* She's frowning. Right away, I can tell something's the matter. Then I see it. She has an envelope in her hand. A telegram! The organ begins to play."

"Frankie, there's no organ in school."

"No, listen! Mrs. Welsby reaches out and, pausing ever so slightly, she offers the telegram to Miss Gomez. The lovely Miss Gomez pales. After a moment of painful hesitation, she rips the telegram open.

Zzzzzt! She gasps. *Aurggg!* Her face goes chalky white. Whish. . . . I could see her heart pounding. Bump. Bump. Her left you-know-what bouncing."

"Oh, God. . . ."

"No. It's true! Little beads of sweat break out on her beautifully formed but trembling red, moist lips. She sits down. *Umph!* She starts to cry. The tears trickle down her face. Drop. Drop. Music swells.

"Knowing what I must do, I stand up and walk forward. I, wealthy, handsome Chet Barker, student-about-town, move forward calmly and say, 'Miss Gomez, has one of your loved ones passed to the great beyond?' "

"You *said* that?"

"Well, close. And she says—"

"Frankie, I don't want to hear."

"No, listen."

"I don't want to hear!"

"She whispers, all throaty, 'Oh, God.' "

"Geez. . . ."

"Mario . . ."

"What?"

"It's seven-thirty."

"So what?"

"Time for 'The Lone Ranger.' "

⚡

"A fiery horse with the speed of light. A cloud of dust and a hearty 'Hi-yo, Silver!' The Lone Ranger rides again!

"With his faithful Indian companion, Tonto, the daring and resourceful masked rider of the plains led the fight for law and order in the early western United States. Nowhere in the pages of history can one find a greater champion of justice.

"Return with us now to those thrilling days of yesteryear. From out of the past come the hoofbeats of the great horse Silver. The Lone Ranger rides again!"

"Come on, Silver! Let's go, big fellow! Hi-yo, Silver, away!"

"At the end of yesterday's episode Bud Titus stormed out of Sheriff Whalen's office. As he walked from town, fuming to himself, he began to realize how much his fit of temper had cost him. Not only had he quit a job he liked, he had also upset his plans to wed Mary Simpson, the daughter of a wealthy rancher. As we join him today, he has decided to go to Mary and tell her everything."

"Mary, the sheriff said I could get my badge back when I cooled off. It'll be mighty humiliating to go back. But if you say I should—"

"Not until after you've proved yourself, Bud. And I think I can help you."

"How?"

"Early this morning Dad and his ranch crew went to the north range to round up strays. I rode along with them just for the exercise. On the way back I saw two men eating by a campfire and I was sure one of them was wearing a mask."

''Think they were Tipsy Malone and Todd
Farrell, those two polecats I let slip through
my fingers?''

''It could be.''

''I'll hide my horse in the brush and go on
foot to take them.''

''Do be careful, Bud.''

''The Lone Ranger and Tonto were saddling
their horses when a voice spoke sharply and Bud
came out from behind the trees.''

''Stand where you are!''

''Kemo sabe, man with gun!''

''Get your hands up! Both of you!''

''Do what he says, Tonto.''

''Ah.''

''That's it. Now keep 'em high. Ha—ha! Well,
you're not the two I expected, but you'll do for
the time being. Here! I'll just take your guns,
mister.''

''Are we riding to town?''

''I am, but you're not. I'll ride that big
white stallion. Whoa, there. Whoa, boy.''

''Silver! Jump!''

''Hey!''

''*Bang!*''

''Silver's jump make him lose gun!''

''Right, Tonto. Now, get to your feet,
Titus.''

''Pretty smart, getting your horse to help.
What do you intend to do with me?''

''After I unload your gun, Bud, I'll let you
go.''

"Let me go? After I tried to shoot you?"

"You thought you were doing your duty. Here's your gun."

"I don't savvy this."

"When you get back to town, give this to the sheriff. He'll explain."

"A bullet? A silver bullet?"

"And, Bud, don't try sneaking back here. Tonto and I will be watching."

"The chagrined Bud Titus headed back to town. But meanwhile, Tipsy Malone and Todd Farrell, the two outlaws, were riding his way when Tipsy stopped suddenly."

"Whoa, boy. Well, Todd, look who's up ahead."

"Why, it's Bud Titus, that tin star who booted us out of town."

"Rein up, mister."

"What!"

"Put your hands up."

"I guess you recognize us, don't you, Tin Star?"

"Yeah, I know you. Murdering polecats."

"Climb down off that horse and be quick about it. Take his gun, Todd. Got it? Now search him. He might have another one."

"Hey, Tipsy, take a look at this silver bullet."

"What! Where were you when a masked man gave you that bullet?"

"It's none of your business where I was."

"Indian with him? Indian named Tonto?"

"Yes, but . . . No, I mean to say . . . Well, go ahead. You got all you want from me. Why don't you shoot me?"

"Not just yet. Todd, take the rope off his saddle. We'll tie him up and leave him here, then follow the trail back and find that masked man."

"Right."

"Sheriff Whalen was still on the lookout for the two outlaws when he came upon Mary Simpson. She told the sheriff how Bud had gone after the two men she had seen."

"But a few moments ago I heard a shot and I'm afraid he—"

"Mary, he shouldn't have gone after those men alone. He should have come into town for me."

"Sheriff, we've got to do something."

"I'll ride out and see what's happening."

"I'll come with you."

"Help! Help!"

"It's Bud, Sheriff! I know his voice."

"Whoa! What happened, Bud? Who tied you up?"

"I'll tell you while you cut these ropes. But hurry."

"Meanwhile, Tipsy Malone and Todd Farrell had followed Bud's trail back."

"There's the campfire, Tipsy. And hoofprints of two horses. The big ones must have been made by that white stallion."

"But they're gone. What'll we do now?"

"Pick up their trail and follow 'em."

"Get your hands up!"

"What the—?"

"Tipsy, behind you! The masked man!"

"You won't get me. Shoot him, Todd!"

"Bang! Bang! Bang! Bang! Bang! Bang! Bang! Bang! Bang!"

"Meanwhile, as Sheriff Whalen and Mary Simpson cut the ropes that bound him, Bud Titus told his story. But the old sheriff had been strangely quiet during Bud's recital of his adventures."

"Bud, I'm afraid you made another mistake, and a mighty big one this time."

"A mistake, Sheriff? I don't understand."

"Hey, listen! Gunshots!"

"Sounds like we might be too late. Get mounted! But whatever you do, don't shoot the masked man or the Indian. Now, keep under cover. Mary, you keep behind us."

"Look! There they are. All four of those crooks."

"Ha—ha! Look again, Bud."

"Hey! The masked man and the Indian have made the other two prisoners!"

"Hello, Sheriff."

"Well, I see you got the ornery mavericks."

"As a matter of fact, Tonto and I were getting ready to ride into town and turn them over to you."

"I'll be glad to take them off your hands right here. I knew those two would ambush you if they got a chance."

"They might have done that if it hadn't been for Bud."

"How's that?"

"When we let Bud go, I thought he might try to come back and take us prisoners again. So Tonto and I moved back into the timber a ways."

"Then we see Malone and Farrell come looking for us."

"The rest was easy."

"Well, they aren't the first outlaws to learn it's not healthy to draw a gun on you."

"Sheriff, I think Bud has learned a lot in the last twenty—four hours."

"Yup. I agree with you. How about it, Bud?"

"Believe me, Sheriff, I'll never make the same fool mistakes again."

"Well, Tonto and I will be going along. Adios, Sheriff!"

"Adios, mister."

"Say, Sheriff, who was that masked man, any— way?"

"Why, Mary, that masked man is the Lone Ranger."

"What the . . . ?"

"The Lone Ranger!"

"Hi—yo, Silver, away!"

"FRANKIE, I think you better go home now. If your mother finds out you're here and learns about that board and if she tells my ma—"

"Mario, who do you like better—Iceman, the Green Hornet, or the Lone Ranger?"

"Iceman. *Nothing* hurts him."

"Fang-toothed tigers can."

"Still, he wins."

"Iceman's okay. But I really *love* the Lone Ranger. I mean, he was a real person. And that mask. . . . Nobody knows who he is. You know what's the best part?"

"What?"

"Right at the end, when someone always says, 'Hey, who was that masked man, anyway?' That's so swell."

"It's dumb."

"Isn't!"

"Sure, it is. If he's supposed to be so famous, how come people never know who he is?"

"The Lone Ranger wants to keep his true identity secret."

"Tonto knows."

"Tonto is his sidekick. Real heroes are *always* secret. I mean, that's almost the whole point of being a hero! Nobody knows they are heroes."

"It's past eight, Frankie. My mother will be coming and . . . Go on. The board's still up."

"Wait a minute. One more thing."

"What?"

"Did you do your English?"

"Frankie? Frankie!"

"It's your mother, Frankie. Better get back!"

"I'm going. What is it, Ma?"

"Where are you?"

"Working on my English!"

"Come down here. Right away!"

"What's the matter?"

"Your father needs to talk to you. He's in the kitchen eating supper."

"Did I get into school trouble?"

"What?"

"Never mind."

"Just go in."

"Could you just tell me what I did?"

"Nothing! This is family business."

"'Lo, Pop."

"Oh, there you are. You tell him yet?"

"No. You should."

"Tell me what?"

"It's about Tom."

"Did Tom get killed?"

"Blessed Mary! What a thing!"

"Ma, I'm just asking."

"Frankie, look at me."

"I am looking, Pop."

"We got an army notification today. Tom's coming home this week."

"Oh, wow!"

"Now listen to me, young man. You know your brother was wounded."

"Did you find out how it happened? Did he capture some prisoners? Or save someone? How many medals did they give him?"

"Relax, Frankie. Relax. We don't know much. His

wound may be bad. Or only something small. They didn't tell us."

"And I was too afraid to ask."

"Aw, Ma!"

"But whatever it is, Frankie, he's going to need plenty of rest."

"And quiet. And we're going to treat him special. He deserves that."

"I know."

"Tom's done what he needed to do, and we have to make sure things are good for him. He's a hero."

"I just said I *know* that, Pop!"

"Now, to begin with, we're giving him your room."

"My *what*?"

"Your room."

"But—"

"We can't turn Mr. Swerdlow out. We need the money. That leaves your room."

"But that's not fair."

"We're not talking fair. We're talking what we're doing. Your brother needs a private place."

"Where am I going to sleep?"

"The basement."

"The basement!"

"I'll fix it up."

"Pop, there's nothing but junk down there. And water when it rains. And it stinks when it gets hot. And roaches and coal dust! Besides, I think Tom would rather have his own room."

"Frankie, this is the way it's going to be."

"What if Mr. Swerdlow moves out?"

"We don't want that."

"But Pop, what if—just *suppose*—he does?"

"Then—if we don't rent it again—Tom can have his room and you can have yours. Frankie, your brother has made a whole lot of sacrifices. For us. For the world. This is the least you can do. Now, what's the matter?"

"One thing. Can I have the radio? When my punishment week is up, I mean."

"Frankie, I think Tom will want it."

"But what about all my programs?"

"Well, if Tom doesn't care—"

"But he *will*."

"Franklin Delano Wattleson! You should be ashamed of yourself!"

"Ma, it's like a dungeon down there. I'll wither away."

"Don't exaggerate."

"Don't I have *any* choice?"

"No."

"Can I ask just one more thing?"

"What?"

"Can I eat a bowl of *POW!* before I go to bed?"

" 'LO, MR. SWERDLOW."

"Oh, hello, Frankie. Didn't see you in the dark there. You're up late, aren't you?"

"I wanted to tell you the news."

"What news is that?"

"My brother, Tom, is coming home."

"Oh, good. Glad to hear it."

"He got terribly wounded."

"Did he?"

"See, he captured this island single-handed. So I think Tom learned a lot in the last few months."

"I'm sure."

"There's one thing he hasn't learned, though."

"What's that?"

"He can't have his room back. I guess that's the price he's paid for the relentless fight of one man against the forces of evil."

"I'm sure he'll adjust."

"I'm giving him my room. I'm going to the basement."

"That's nice of you."

"Mr. Swerdlow, if you wanted to, you could move down to the basement instead of me. You could have it for nine dollars and ten cents a week. In one year you'd have saved . . . Well, it's a lot."

"Frankie, I like it where I am."

"There's a lot more room there. It's the most private place in the whole house. No one goes there. And then Tom could have his own room."

"Frankie, you're going to have to excuse me. I've some studying to do."

"Mr. Swerdlow! My brother has made a whole lot

of sacrifices. For us. For the world! It's the least you can do!"

"Good-night, Frankie."

"I warn you, I intend to lead the fight for law and order in this house!"

"Episode 3"

"CHET BARKER, Master Spy!"

"Da-dum, da-dum!"

"Shredded Oat Cakes brings you another thrilling adventure of Chet Barker, Master Spy! Chet Barker, ruthless, clear-eyed, cunning, and full of potential. Chet Barker, thundering out of the dim past in a constant search for his true identity! Chet Barker, fighting hand to hand for what's right. On the land!"

"On the sea!"

"And in the air! Da-dum! With his faithful but eccentric sidekick, Skipper O'Malley, Chet Barker *believes* in the American way!"

"Da-dum!"

"And now for today's adventure. It's called Into the Dungeon! As we discover our young heroes, they are heading down the back stairs. I say, 'Look out for boa constrictors, Skip.' You say, 'I'm a watching, Chet.' "

"I'm a watching, Chet."

"Bullets whine. *Ping! Ping!* You say, 'I don't like this, Chet.' "

"I don't like this, Chet."

"I say, 'Keep her steady, Skip.' You say, 'I'm a trying, Chet.' "

"I'm a trying, Chet."

"I see the door. It's covered with snot."

"That's disgusting, Frankie!"

"That's the whole point!"

"They wouldn't do that on the radio. And my mother doesn't want me to be disgusting."

"Come on, Mario."

"But it's *really* disgusting."

"We going to do this or not?"

"I just want to see your new room."

"Okay, the door is covered with slime."

"That's better."

"I say, 'Brace yourself.' You say, 'I'm a doing it.' "

"Frankie, what's all this 'a' stuff?"

"That's the way sidekicks talk!"

"You never said so before."

"Mario, you ruin everything! Okay, there, see."

"Oh, wow. You really going to live here?"

"Have to clean it up. Does have one great thing, though."

"What?"

"Coal chute."

"What's so great about that?"

"We can use it as a secret entrance."

"It's too filthy."

"That's the whole point. No one else would think of using it."

"So much junk. . . . What are these lists?"

"I don't know."

"All these names. Shoo-in. Bright Wind. Galloping Gold. Silver Blast. With numbers after them. What's it mean?"

"Codes."

"What kind of codes?"

"Secret ones, I suppose. Yeah, a G-man once lived here."

"Sure, sure. But what do they *mean*?"

"Mario, if they weren't secret, they wouldn't be codes, right?"

"Well . . ."

"So if they *are* codes, that means it's secret, right? And if it's a secret, that means I can't tell you, right?"

"You know what? I just figured out something."

"What?"

"Whenever you don't know an answer, you say, 'It's a secret.' "

"Makes it more interesting."

"Hey, Frankie, with you down here we won't be able to talk much."

"Sure, we can. I just sent off for a Silver Fox Junior G-man Walkie-talkie."

"You did?"

"Four Corn Cracks box tops and thirty-five cents."

"I hate Corn Cracks."

"Me too."

"You had to eat it, though."

"Naw. I flushed most of it down the toilet."

"Didn't your mother get mad?"

"Think I did it with her standing there?"

"When's Tom coming?"

"Any day. I asked Mr. Swerdlow to give his room back to him, but he won't."

"Pays rent, doesn't he?"

"I know. But I really need to get him out. And I will too. . . ."

"All this stuff. . . . What's that?"

"Boxes."

"No, that."

"I don't know. . . . Oh, wow, gee whiz, Mario, look. A radio!"

"Well, maybe."

"I'm sure it is!"

"I'm not."

"It is! Look!"

"Well, if it is, it's old. All these dials. This must be the speaker. Only it's separate."

"I don't care. Think it'll work?"

"Don't know."

"Mario, you can fix it. I know you can."

"This stuff all right to fool with?"

"I'll go ask my pop."

"POP?"

"What's that?"

"In the basement there's all this stuff."

"What stuff?"

"Radio stuff."

"Radio stuff? Oh, yeah. Belonged to your uncle Charley."

"Pop, did I ever know Uncle Charley?"

"He was your mother's brother."

"Yeah, but did I ever *see* him?"

"Once. Maybe. I'm not sure."

"Is he dead?"

"No."

"Where'd he go, then?"

"What is this, 'The Answer Man'?"

"But if he's gone, can I have his things? Can I? Please?"

"Frankie, don't bother me. Can't you see how tired I am?"

"WHAT DID HE SAY?"

"Said I wasn't supposed to bother him."

"What's that mean?"

"That's what grown-ups say when they don't know the answer. Think you can get it to work?"

"With this speaker not being part of the set, I don't know. . . . Boy, I don't like this place."

"Good training."

"For what?"

"Being locked up in jail. You know what I think?"

"What?"

"See that broken wire? And that one?"

"Yeah . . ."

"I bet they attach here."

"Frankie, I don't think so."

"Sure, they do."

"Frankie, you're going to blow a fuse or something."

"Mario, the only way to know if things work is to plug 'em in."

"I'm not so sure."

"Well, I am. Here goes. Anything happening?"

"It's starting to smoke. Frankie! Unplug!"

"Shhh!"

"Frankie? That you down there?"

"It's your father!"

"Shhh. Don't worry."

"What's going on down there?"

"Just me and Mario."

"What's that smell?"

"I don't know."

"You kids smoking?"

"No."

"Okay. Guess it's gone."

"Mario?"

"What?"

"I think we better take the stuff over to your place. And besides . . ."

"What?"

"I don't want to miss 'Hop Harrigan.' "

"Episode 4"

"MA! HE'S HERE! Ma! It's Tom!"

"Oh, my God!"

"Ma! Hurry! He's outside!"

"I'm coming! I'm coming!"

"This the Wattleson residence, kiddo?"

"Yes, sir."

"Home of Private First Class Thomas Peter Wattleson?"

"Sure is."

"Where is he? I'm Mrs. Wattleson."

"He's right here, ma'am. Doing just fine. We've got him right here. You his mother?"

"Yes, sir."

"Great."

"Is he all right? What's the matter? Can't he walk? Oh, God. . . ."

"Just a moment, ma'am. Hold on. He's doing great. We'll give him a hand. Come on, soldier. You made it, pal. You're home."

"Hello, Ma. Hi, Frankie."

"Tom! Oh, Tom!"

"THANKS for letting me have your room, kid."

"That's okay."

"Yeah, buddy, good to be home. You don't know."

"But I bet you'd be happier in your own room, wouldn't you?"

"Don't worry about it, kiddo. Just glad to be here, that's all."

"It's a lot bigger up there. And the third floor is higher. Better air."

"This is fine, Frankie. Anyway, Ma said someone was renting my old room."

"Mr. Swerdlow. Tom, guess what? He's probably an evil scientist. Or maybe in the rackets."

"The rackets?"

"I'm beginning to suspect so."

"Why?"

"Just do."

"Did you tell Pop?"

"No."

"How come?"

"I'm still sifting the evidence."

"I wouldn't worry about it."

"Tom?"

"What?"

"Do you think the radio will bother you?"

"No. It's fine. Nice to have it. How you getting on?"

"Okay."

"You got bigger."

"I eat a lot of breakfast."

"How's Ma doing?"

"Fine."

"Pop?"

"He's got two jobs. At the box factory. Then at night, sometimes, with Mr. Giorgi, the plumber."

"He told me. How's school?"

"Okay."

"Ma said you got a new pal who moved in right next door."

"Yeah. Mario Calvino. He lives right there. We're in the same class. He's very scientific. And his father got killed in the war."

"I heard. . . . Ma says the only thing you're interested in is your radio programs. That true?"

"I'm interested in other things."

"Like what?"

"Heroes. You ever hear of the Lone Ranger?"

"Sure."

"He's so swell. Wears a mask. . . ."

"Kiddo, you going to just stare at me all the time?"

"No."

"Come on, pal. Rest easy."

"Tom?"

"What?"

"Did it hurt a lot?"

"For a while."

"Will you be able to walk again?"

"Yeah. Specially with the cane."

"Then how come you don't?"

"Not interested in going anywhere."

"Tom . . ."

"What?"

"What was it like?"

"What?"

"Getting hit."

"Frankie, I don't want to talk about it."

"Was it exciting? Did you get creased? Would you show me the wound? I never saw one."

"Frankie . . ."

"Everybody *says* you're a hero."

"Forget it."

"Would you . . . Could you tell me about it? What it was like and all. And Mario wants to meet you. And your leg."

"Don't think I want to see anyone for a while."

"You don't?"

"Later, maybe. Hey, what about school? Still at good old P.S. Eight?"

"Sixth grade."

"Who's your teacher?"

"Miss Gomez."

"Wasn't there when I was. You like her?"

"She looks like Veronica Lake, but you know what? Lately, she's been troubled a lot about me. Think you could visit school and tell her not to worry about me so much?"

"Nope."

"Guess what? Her boyfriend got killed."

"Oh. You working hard in school?"

"No."

"Why not?"

"It's boring. Tom?"

"What?"

"Can I ask you something really, really personal?"

"Depends."

"It's important. Really."

"Shoot."

"Who do you like better—Iceman, Captain Midnight, or the Lone Ranger?"

"POP?"

"Frankie, can't you see your father's reading the paper?"

"I have to ask him something."

"He's tired."

"That's okay. What is it, Frankie?"

"It's about Tom."

"What about him?"

"Is something the matter with him?"

"You wouldn't be in so great a mood if your leg got hurt like that."

"Was he shot anywhere else?"

"What do you mean?"

"Well, his head. . . ."

"What the hell you saying?"

"He's a hero, right?"

"Sure."

"How come he doesn't talk like one? And how come he doesn't want to see anyone?"

"Frankie, do everybody a favor and leave your father alone. And go do your homework."

"Ma, I'm trying to talk to Pop."

"You know we got a letter from your school."

"You did?"

"From your teacher. She said you never do your schoolwork. And that all you do is talk about radio shows. Says she's tired of making you stay after. And if you keep messing up, she's going to have to do something drastic."

"I know, Ma."

"That all you can say?"

"Pop, did you like school?"

"I never stayed past seventh grade."

"How come?"

"My folks were hard up. I had to go to work."

"You were lucky."

"Think so?"

"I never heard of one hero who went to school. Ever."

"Frankie, let me tell you something straight. Now listen. You're *lucky* to be in school. Think about the kids in France. Or Russia. What kind of schooling they got? So, I'm telling you, if you get into bad trouble in school—long as I'm your father, long as your mother is your mother—no radio. *Ever*. What do you have to say to that?"

"Real heroes have no parents."

"Episode 5"

"FRANKIE, come up to my place. I got to show you something."

"What?"

"About your uncle's old radio stuff."

"You get it working?"

"I'll show you."

"Your mother home? I don't think she'd want to know."

"She's doing a late shift. Won't be home for hours."

"Okay."

"FRANKIE, I've been looking at this junk from your basement, and you know what? I don't think it's a radio."

"What is it?"

"More like something for getting or sending messages by wire."

"Oh, wow!"

"Why would your uncle Charley be sending messages?"

"I'm beginning to think he was a brilliant but eccentric scientist."

"Really?"

"Well, he did disappear. That's what usually happens to brilliant but eccentric scientists."

"Think he was evil?"

"Probably works for the government."

"Where do you think he went?"

"Atop some remote mountain hideaway."

"Doing what?"

"Inventing something. Like a sleep generator. It puts war criminals into a hypnotic trance, clouds their minds, and makes them confess automatically."

"Oh, gee!"

"Yeah, he's smart. Like you. Think you can get any of this stuff to work?"

"That's what I was trying to say. It sort of *does* work."

"It does?"

"Well, see, when I talk into this part, the voice goes out that part."

"It does?"

"In a way."

"Show me."

"Take this—it's the speaker. Now, trail out that wire into the front room. Go on."

"Like this?"

"Yeah. Okay. Now put your ear close up to it. Ready? Okay, this is Skipper, calling Chet! Can you hear me, Chet?"

"Hey, swell, Mario, it works! So nifty! The best ever! We'll run wires from here to my place in the basement. Then I'll be able to get radio programs down there when you put your radio on up here."

"I guess."

"Can you make it any louder?"

"Don't think so."

"Mario, you know something? You really are an actual genius. I mean, if you ever became an *evil* genius, the whole world would be in trouble. Only thing is, we have to give it a name."

"What about Radio Sender?"

"Has to be better than that. I know! We'll call it an Atomic Radio Remote Relay."

"I don't get it."

"It sends radio voices."

"What's the atomic part?"

"That's just a way of saying it's in the future."

"There is a problem: it works only one way. How am I going to know when you want me to turn the radio on?"

"We can use my Silver Fox Junior G-man Walkie-talkie set."

"When's it coming?"

"Soon."

"You've been saying that. . . ."

"Don't worry. It'll get here. Come on. There's a ton of wire down in my basement. If we can set this up before your ma gets back, I can listen to 'Sky King.' "

"And now, 'Sky King'!"

"You remember what happened, don't you? Sky King, Penny, Clipper, Martha, and Jim Bell had managed to get across the river with the yelling, shouting giants close at their heels. Sky tried to cut down the bridge, but the blade of his knife broke. Then, with long deadly spears whistling through the air, with the giants screaming at their backs, Sky and our friends ran into the forest. There they heard the bridge go down, heard the giants as they fell into the river, saw ahead of them—an army of blue men!

"Now, with the frenzied howls of the giants echoing in their ears and the blue men coming to-ward them too, Sky King speaks."

"Quick, behind these bushes."

"Sky, what are we going to do? There're hun-dreds of those blue guys!"

"They might not be looking for us, but for

those giants yelling down there. Maybe they'll
go down to the river to investigate. If they
don't, they ain't human.''

''But look at them, Sky. All blue! Even their
hands and their hair.''

''Me, I ain't caring what color they are. Long
as they stay away from us.''

''Hey! They're going down the banks. They're
going down to the river, Sky!''

''Wish we could hear what they were saying. We
might find out what gives with those blue boys.
If they're looking for us. . . .''

''Gosh. How could they be, Sky? How could they
know we're here?''

''Maybe King Ramses has been able to keep a
close track on our movements.''

''Are we in his country, Sky? Is this the Land
of the Diamond Scarab?''

''That's how I'm betting it, Penny.''

''Where we going now, Sky?''

''Find a better place to hide in, honey.
Around here, between those giants and the blue
boys, it's more crowded than a department store
two days before Christmas. How about it, Jim?
See anybody on that hill?''

''The whole no-good lot of them are down at
the river.''

''For me, I don't wish them bad luck or nothing, but I kind of hope a big crocodile takes a
nip out of a couple of 'em.''

''You might get your wish, Martha.''

"Let's make it to the top of this hill. From there we can at least see those birds if they come up this way. Everybody ready?"

"Yes, Sky, I sure am."

"All right. Easy does it now. No running. Stay in the brush as much as possible. That's the way. We're getting to the top here."

"Phew! I'm hot!"

"Better loosen your tie, Clipper."

"Hey, Sky. Look below!"

"What?"

"Down the hill!"

"Wha . . . A city. A great big city!"

"With streets."

"And buildings."

"And fountains."

"Look how them fountains glitter."

"Gosh!"

"They're just like diamonds."

"Oh, Sky, do you think they really *are* diamonds?"

"Yes, Penny, I do."

"Them's as big as your head. Bigger!"

"And there's the palace, Sky. It's bigger than all those other buildings. And it's got a big scarab on its roof."

"Well, Clipper, in a little while we're going down there and see if we can find Nancy Campbell."

"We'll never get past all those guards, Sky. They're everywhere."

"But that's why we came to Ecuador, you know, to get Nancy Campbell and Joe Butler out of this place. So try to catch some rest, all of you, because as soon as it gets dark we're going down there."

"Evening wanders across the heavens now. The quick, tropic twilight slides its way over the forest. Night, like a black velvet cloak, wraps itself around the jungle. Sky King and our friends stand on a hill and look down on the lights of a fabulous city, down on the Land of the Diamond Scarab."

"Episode 6"

"HEY, MARIO!"

"What?"

"Look!"

"What is it?"

"It came!"

"What is it?"

"My Silver Fox Junior G-man Walkie-talkie."

"*That?*"

"All you have to do is put it together."

"What's it made of?"

"Cardboard."

"That's no good."

"It's *special* cardboard."

"Looks regular to me."

"You'll see. Here. Put it together. Then we can talk two ways."

"Why don't you put it together?"

"Because I'm always putting tab *A* in slot *B* instead of *C*."

"It's easy."

"Well, you're a better speller than I am."

"HELLO, SKIPPER! Hello! This is Chet Barker calling Skipper O'Malley on the Silver Fox Junior G-man Walkie-talkie. Come in, please. Come in. Use your Atomic Radio Remote Relay to reply. Over and out."

"What?"

"Did you hear me?"

"Louder!"

"Mario, pull the string tighter! The thing won't work unless the string's really tight!"

"Okay!"

"Oh, great, now you *snapped* the string!"

"HELLO, SKIPPER! Come in, please! This is Chet! Roger?"

"Who's Roger?"

"Mario, *roger* means 'I hear you.' "

"Frankie, I can hear you, but it's too faint. Can't we just talk regular?"

"No!"

"Why?"

"Because when you use the Atomic Remote Relay Radio, I don't want to have to run outside to answer each time."

"We could just meet out front, you know."
"People would hear."
"Nobody cares."
"What about our enemies?"
"What enemies?"
"Public enemies, like Mr. Swerdlow."
"Oh, him."
"Come on. Let's get it right."

"THIS IS Chet Barker calling Skipper O'Malley on the walkie-talkie! The string is in place! Repeat! The string is in place! Would you come in, please! Over and roger?"
"What did you say?"
"It works, Mario! We can talk both ways!"
"Great! What's the message?"
"Meet me on the stoop."
"Why?"
"I need your English homework."

"Episode 7"

"SAY, TOM . . . ?"

"What's that, Pop?"

"How about, right after dinner, we take in a movie? There's a new Bob Hope comedy over at the Majestic Theater. Supposed to be good."

"Can I go?"

"Frankie, you have homework to do."

"Aw, Ma, it's Saturday."

"What do you say, Tom? Be good to get out. We can make a night of it. Even take in a beer or two."

"You and Ma go."

"If I did my homework, could I go then?"

"Frankie, you are *not* going!"

"How about it, Tom? Might see some of your old buddies and gals. . . ."

"If Tom goes out, can I listen to the radio in his room?"

"Frankie, keep out of this!"

"Ma!"

"Thanks for the invite, Pop, but I'm not feeling so great. Some other time. I'd just as soon go lie down."

"I wish I understood what was eating that boy up."

"Ma, I know what it is."

"What?"

"It's the music he listens to. It's so dopey. If he listened to adventures, he'd have a lot more pep and energy to be wide awake and husky."

"Frankie, do me a favor?"

"What?"

"Go down to your room and just turn yourself off."

"FRANKIE, you know what? That walkie-talkie thing doesn't work too well."

"If you held the string tighter, it would."

"From my radio down your coal chute is too far."

"Mario, you know something? You give up too easy."

"My ma says all that stuff is junk. She's right too."

"We need it."

"Why?"

"Because somebody has to lead the fight for law

and order around here. And you want to get on the pages of history, don't you?"

"I guess. How's your brother?"

"Okay."

"Still in bed?"

"Sort of."

"Will he see anyone yet?"

"Nope."

"What is he, sick?"

"I think it's the room."

"What do you mean?"

"Being in my room is sort of not being really home yet. So he can't do anything but lie around. Before he went into the army, he'd sit out on the stoop, like we're doing, talking with his friends. Now he won't see anyone or hardly listen to the radio either. And when he does listen, it's all sappy love music."

"My mother gets like that sometimes. It scares me. She just stares at the wall. Like she was reading some message on it."

"Hey, maybe there *is* a message."

"No, there isn't. I looked."

"Oh, hi, Mr. Swerdlow."

"Excuse me, boys. Can I get out?"

"Oh, sure. Hey, Mr. Swerdlow, you going to operate on anybody today?"

"I think not."

"So long."

"Bye. . . ."

"You know what?"

"What?"

"Maybe he's the one made my uncle Charley disappear."

"You said that was years ago."

"I know. Well, anyway, I just got an important clue: Mr. Swerdlow's in the big-time rackets."

"How can you know?"

"The way he talks."

"Talks?"

"You heard him. 'I think not.' That's fancy stuff. Small-time racketeers talk like people from Jersey. Big-time ones sound like England. Hey, come on. Let's follow him."

"Are you nuts?"

"We can match wits with him. See where he goes! I'll get my mask."

"HEY! Where'd you get that?"

"Pearlman's Candy. Nickel a mask."

"Why you wearing your glasses on the outside?"

"So I can see, stupid!"

"You're going to trip on your father's coat, you know. It's too long. That his hat?"

"Yeah. Think anyone will recognize me?"

"Naw. You look more like a walking mushroom than a spy. But what if your father sees you?"

"Have to chance it, Skipper. Now, which way did he go?"

"That way."

"Okay. We're in a South American jungle. It's evening. The very fast twilight zips its way overhead. Night, like a black scarab, settles down. Trees are everywhere. So are these blue, frenzied sloths. And great orange giants are chasing us with huge, slobbering—really hungry—mouths. I say, 'Okay, Skipper, I don't fancy being eaten. Better keep your eyes peeled.' You say, 'Count on me, Chet.' "

"Count on me, Chet. That's disgusting—peeled eyes."

"Mario!"

"Just saying. . . ."

"I say, 'He's right up ahead, Skipper. He thinks we can't see him.' You say, 'Doesn't know what a great tracker you are, Chet.' "

"Doesn't know what a great tracker you are, Chet."

"Learned it from my uncle Charley."

"Thought you said he was an eccentric scientist."

"But first he was a daring World War One flying ace. Part of the Lost Squadron. Anyway, I'm only trying to do my job, Skip. Now, we slip past the quicksand pools, then swim through this alligator-infested river. Suddenly I see this gigantic man-eating crocodile. Da-dum!"

"Thought you said alligators."

"They got all kinds. That's how bad it is. I cry, 'Help! Skipper! He has me by the leg. Arrg!' In a flash you pull the teeth out of your knife and stab him right in his double heart."

"Don't you mean 'pull the knife out of your teeth'?"

"I said that."

"No, you didn't. You said 'teeth out of your knife'!"

"I did not."

"You did!"

"Would you just do the second thing."

"I forgot what the second thing was."

"Okay. Skip it. I say, 'Thanks, pardner. Once again you saved my life.' You say, ' 'Tweren't nothing.' Come on, Mario. . . . Stop laughing!"

"You really did."

"Oh, shut up! Where's Mr. Swerdlow?"

"There."

"Right, Skipper. Keep your eyes peeled."

"I wish you'd just say open."

"If you don't say it right, it won't work."

"But you keep repeating the same things over and over. It's dumb."

"Mario, are you going to make up the words, or me?"

"I can't do it real like you."

"Well?"

"Okay. My eyes are open. Peeled."

"Mario, did you see what I saw?"

"What?"

"Mr. Swerdlow got into a car!"

"So what?"

"He got into the *backseat*! That's where the gang leaders *always* ride."

"Frankie, people were sitting up front. There was no room!"

"By gumption, Skipper, once again the racketeer is saved by the Dark Hand Gang. And so we come to another end of another Chet Barker, Master Spy, adventure."

"With his faithful sidekick, Skipper O'Malley."

"Tune in tomorrow for excitement!"

"Thrills!"

"And adventure! Yes, radio fans, find out tomorrow what happens when Chet Barker and his sidekick, Skipper O'Malley, learn more about the evil Doctor Swerdlow."

"Hey, there goes Miss Gomez."

"Where?"

"There. Down Montague Street."

"Come on! We'll follow her. We're on a secret mission. It's Berlin. Midnight. Sirens are screeching. The artillery has opened up on the advancing Americans. Miss Gomez is a lovely young spy with crucial information for the Allies. The situation is so bad it's desperate. The fate of the entire universe depends on her. Meanwhile, we've parachuted down from a B-17 to protect her!"

"Frankie, can't we just do something normal for once?"

"Come on, Mario! I say, 'Skipper, my heart goes out to her because she's mighty young and innocent for this kind of operation.' You say, 'Well, Chet, a pretty face is a mighty weapon.' "

"Well, Chet, a pretty face is a mighty weapon."

"Then I say, 'Right, Skipper. The look of innocence oft snares the stripling youth.' "

"I don't know what that means."

"Mario, can't you understand *anything*?"

"I know science. I figured how to get the Atomic Radio Remote Relay to work, didn't I? And put the Silver Fox Junior G-man Walkie-talkie together, right?"

"Yeah, but those things were real. This is an adventure. Hey, I bet she's heading toward Penny Bridge Park. Come on!"

"Wait a minute. The stoplight's going to change."

"Mario, heroes don't wait for lights to change! There, see, I told you. She went into the park."

"Frankie, there's nothing else *but* park."

"It's a perfect ron-day-voo place. I say, 'Keep your head down, Skipper. We may be in for it.' You say, 'I read you, Chet.' "

"I read you, Chet. Frankie, she's just sitting there."

"Right. She's waiting."

"Waiting for what?"

"An Allied double agent."

"No, she's not. Frankie, she's . . . she's crying."

"Oh, wow. . . ."

"Yeah."

"Must be about . . ."

"I don't like this. . . . I'm going home."

"Mario!"

"MISS GOMEZ? Miss Gomez!"

"Yes . . . ?"

"Miss Gomez?"

"I . . ."

"You are Miss Gomez, aren't you?"

"Yes. . . . Who are you? Why are you wearing that ridiculous costume? How do you know my name?"

"It's all right, Miss Gomez. Don't despair. The Lost Foreign Force of Forgotten Free French Heroes—the LFFFFH—is watching. Don't despair!"

"I don't understand. What are you trying to spell?"

"Until we meet again . . ."

"Come back here! Who are you? What were you saying?"

"COME IN, Skipper. Come in! Chet Barker calling Skipper. Over and out."

"What?"

"Can you hear me at all?"

"What?"

"Keep the string tight, Mario!"

"I'm trying. What happened with you and Miss Gomez?"

"I spoke to her."

"*You did?*"

"Sure."

"Meet me out front."

"WERE YOU *really* wearing your mask and all?"

"Chet Barker never reveals his true identity."

"No fins?"

"No fins."

"No crossed veins?"

"No crossed veins."

"Cross your heart and hope to die?"

"Cross my heart and hope to die."

"Swear on your mother?"

"On my mother."

"What did you say to her?"

"I said the LFFFFH was watching over her."

"The *what?*"

"The Foreign Legion Force of Forgotten French Heroes."

"You said LFFFFH."

"What's the difference?"

"Frankie, it doesn't work out right. The-T, Foreign-F, Legion-L—"

"Come on, Mario!"

"What else did you say to her?"

"That we're going to look after her."

"We are?"

"The F and so on. That's what heroes do, help people in distress."

"Maybe she can help herself."

"Mario, if people could help themselves, they wouldn't have invented heroes, right? She needs Chet Barker. And you, Skipper O'Malley, my faithful sidekick."

"How we going to do it?"

"On the way home I figured out a whole plot."

"You did?"

"One of the things heroes do is get the guy and the girl together, right?"

"Yeah. . . ."

"So, first, I figured that if we could get Miss Gomez married with Tom, he wouldn't be so unhappy."

"But you said he doesn't want to see anybody."

"I'll figure something. Okay, after they get together, since she'd be my relative, I wouldn't get into any school trouble."

"How come?"

"Her husband—that would be Tom—wouldn't let her treat me bad. But here's the best part. See, they couldn't get married unless they had a place to live, right? Okay, so they would *have* to get out of my room because it's too small. Okay? Well, that means they would want to move into *Tom's* old room. Because it's bigger. Except that means we have to get Mr. Swerdlow out *first*, which is good. Because if Tom and Miss Gomez get married, they wouldn't have time to do much except, you know, talk to each other and, you know, stuff."

"Oh, wow!"

"So, the way the adventure ends is, I get the radio."

"Frankie, that's so neat. How did you get it so it works like that?"

"Miss Gomez says I have a lot of potential."

"I wish I could make up stories like that."

"This isn't merely a story, Skipper. It's what every real red-blooded American boy wants. A chance to help others in a selfless quest for justice and the triumph of the Allied forces, because nowhere in the pages of history can one find greater champions of justice. Are you with me?"

"I don't know. . . ."

"I tell you, Skipper, this will be our toughest case. Crack this one, and every public enemy in America will live in constant fear. But wait a minute!"

"What?"

" 'Green Hornet' time."

''The Green Hornet!

''He hunts the biggest of all game, public enemies who try to destroy our America.

''With his faithful valet, Kato, Britt Reid,
daring young publisher, matches wits with the
underworld, risking his life that criminals and
racketeers within the law may feel its weight by
the sting of the Green Hornet!

''This program is brought to you by the makers

of Ovaltine, the famous food drink that is a favorite with millions of Americans, young and
old. Ovaltine is a favorite food drink for two
reasons. First, because it's so downright good.
You'll love its rich, satisfying flavor. So different from any other drink you ever tasted. And
you'll never grow tired of it. Second, because
Ovaltine is so good for you. It brings you loads
and loads of valuable vitamins, minerals, and
other vital food elements that help build
strong, healthy bodies, gives you the pep and energy to be wide awake and husky.

"So tell Mother you'd like to start drinking
Ovaltine every single day.

"And now, ride with Britt Reid in the thrilling adventure Woman in the Case! The Green Hornet strikes again!"

"SAY, TOM?"

"What's that?"

"How come you're always just lying back on your
bed, listening to that love-stuff music and smoking
cigarettes?"

"I like it."

"But it's kind of . . . sappy, isn't it?"

"It's okay."

"You know, 'The Lone Ranger' has great music."

"This is okay."

"Does your leg still hurt?"

"A bit."

"That still the reason you don't go anywhere or see anyone?"

"I just don't feel like it."

"You know what you could do?"

"What?"

"Put a sword in your crutch."

"A what?"

"A sword. In case you get attacked."

"The war's there, Frankie. Not here."

"What about guys in the rackets?"

"Oh, sure. . . ."

"They're all around us, you know."

"If you say so."

"I mean, like Mr. Swerdlow—"

"Frankie, nothing's wrong with Mr. Swerdlow."

"Tom, did you ever talk to him?"

"Sure."

"Well?"

"He's just an ordinary guy."

"That's only what he wants you to think. Tom?"

"What?"

"I wish you'd tell me what it was like."

"What's that?"

"You know . . . the war and all."

"Sometime."

"Steve Trentman's dad just got out of the army. Nelly Ubell's did too. He was telling the kids all about it. Really neat stuff too. About—"

"Come on, kiddo, scoot. I want to listen to this music."

"Tom?"

"What?"

"Can I ask you one more thing? Something really important."

"Depends."

"Do you have a woman in the case?"

"A what?"

"You know, a girlfriend."

"Frankie, do me a favor and get lost."

"I mean, some heroes are allowed to have one, right?"

"Go."

"Iceman has one, Pixy Fontane. Tom, you know what I figured out? He's twelve thousand one hundred and twenty-one years older than she is, and they get along swell."

"Out!"

"Episode 8"

"ALL RIGHT, class. Today, in geography, we're going to start a whole new project. As I told you, each of you will pick a country and do a project on it. Remember, I asked you to read in your geography books and think about which country you'd like to do. Perhaps some of you have already made up your minds. Yes, Henry?"

"Can I do Russia?"

"Well, yes. One of our allies. What makes you interested in Russia?"

"I like Russia."

"Well, then, good idea. Yes, Bette?"

"Can I do Mexico?"

"Our next-door neighbor. And what makes you want to do Mexico, Bette?"

"It's warm there. I don't like being cold."

"Fine. Franklin! Nice to see your hand up. What country would you like?"

"Transylvania."

"Transylvania?"

"Yeah."

"Franklin, I believe Transylvania is a region of Romania, not a country."

"But that's where Dracula comes from."

"Class! Franklin Wattleson, you may go stand in the corner."

"And its principal product is blood."

"And you will stay after school."

"FRANKLIN . . ."

"Yes, Miss Gomez."

"What am I going to do with you?"

"I don't know."

"Franklin, if your behavior doesn't improve—and improve fast—I'll tell you what's going to happen."

"What?"

"You're going to repeat sixth grade."

"You mean . . . be left back?"

"Yes, left back."

"Oh."

"How do you think your parents would feel if I called them and told them that?"

"I told you—we don't have a phone."

"I could always visit."

"If you did, it would be a good time for me to haul my freight out of here."

"Where do you get these expressions?"

"Radio."

"Franklin, I am trying to talk to you seriously."

"If I got left back, would you be my teacher again?"

"Not likely."

"Why?"

"Franklin, I want you to consider what I've been saying. It's important. Being left back means a whole year wasted. You don't want to get stuck, do you? Life will pass you by. People should move ahead. Accept disappointments and look to the future. Now I want you to think about that for a moment, then tell me your thoughts."

"Miss Gomez?"

"Yes?"

"I've thought about it."

"That was very quick."

"Can I ask you something?"

"That depends. . . ."

"It's about accepting disappointments and looking to the future."

"Fine. What about it?"

"Do you have another boyfriend yet?"

"Franklin!"

"Do you?"

"Franklin Wattleson, do you *want* me to visit your parents?"

"Well . . ."

"Then not *another* word!"

"Miss Gomez?"

"Franklin, I'm trying to grade papers."

"Can I speak?"

"Is it important?"

"The fate of the entire universe depends on it."

"Go ahead, then."

"Maybe I could get my parents to call you. Then you wouldn't have to visit."

"Do you think they would call?"

"If I said you wanted them to."

"I'd be happy to talk to them. They can reach me here, at school, after three."

"They both work."

"I thought it was just your father."

"My mother's thinking about the war effort."

"I suppose I could give you my home number."

"It would save you a visit. . . ."

"Very well, I will."

"FRANKIE, why are you home so late?"

"Miss Gomez kept me after school."

"It's nice you come home to sleep. . . ."

"You know what, Ma? I think she likes talking to me."

"Don't flatter yourself."

"Honest. She does. Because she's a lonely, desperate woman and I think she finds me interesting."

"Frankie!"

"I take her mind off what's bothering her."

"What's bothering her?"

"Her boyfriend got killed. Can I ask you something?"

"What?"

"How'd you meet Pop?"

"What kind of a question is that?"

"I'm curious."

"We were introduced."

"By who?"

"My brother."

"Uncle Charley?"

"Yes."

"Ma?"

"What?"

"What happened to Uncle Charley?"

"Nothing."

"Did Mr. Swerdlow have anything to do with it?"

"Don't be absurd."

"Well, then, where'd Uncle Charley go?"

"Somewhere."

"I know that. But *where*?"

"Curiosity killed the cat."

"Satisfaction brought him back. Is he dead?"

"I don't believe so."

"Think he'll ever come here again?"

"I . . . I don't know."

"You don't? Why?"

"Frankie . . ."

"Ma, please tell me! In the basement—the wires

and the radio stuff, and the codes—was he on some secret mission? Or . . . he wasn't an enemy spy, was he?"

"Franklin! Don't even *think* such a thing!"

"Just asking."

"Frankie, please go and do your homework."

"You want to know what I think? I think telling me to do homework is your way of saying you don't want to answer me. What are you making?"

"Apple dumplings."

"Can I have one?"

"When I'm done. Now, just go."

"MARIO, we've got to act fast."

"About what?"

"Our plot. I'm going to be in big trouble if we don't."

"How come?"

"Miss Gomez is going to leave me back. She even gave me her number so my parents could call her."

"Did they?"

"You crazy? Think I'd give her number to them?"

"Come on, Frankie, she didn't give you her number."

"Here it is."

"I bet you stole it."

"I did not!"

"Frankie, adults don't like it when kids mess around with them."

"You know what your problem is, Mario?"

"What?"

"You don't have faith in the American way."

"I do too!"

"The American way means fighting for what's important. And it's important that I have my own radio, right? Well, I just have to work harder."

"What are you going to do?"

"Skipper, I've been doing some snooping around. Laying the groundwork. But now, it's time."

"Time for what?"

"Time to go down to Pearlman's so we can telephone Miss Gomez."

"Are you kidding?"

"Skipper, I don't reckon I've ever been more serious in my whole life. The future of the entire universe is at stake."

"IT'S HOT in this phone booth."

"Mario, just give me that nickel."

"Frankie, you're going to get us into terrible trouble."

"Heroes take chances. Shhh! It's ringing."

"Hello?"

"Is this Miss Gomez?"

"Yes."

"This is the French Force of Lost Foreign and Forgotten Heroes. The F-F . . . Mario!"

"L."

"L."
"F."
"F."
"F."
"F."
"H."
"H."
"The what? Who is this?"
"Chet Barker, Masked Avenger."
"Who?"
"Don't worry. We still intend to help!"
"Help what?"
"Accept disappointment and look—"
"What happened?"
"She hung up."
"Frankie, I feel sick. I'm going home."

"Episode 9"

"OH, HI, Mr. Swerdlow."

"Good evening, Frankie."

"Think it'll rain?"

"Not a cloud in the sky, Frankie."

"Don't be fooled, Mr. Swerdlow. A storm could strike just as quick and deadly as the Silver Fox."

"Ah . . . good-night."

"Mr. Swerdlow?"

"Yes, Frankie."

"Want me to carry your package?"

"Thanks. I can manage."

"CHET BARKER calling sidekick Skipper O'Malley! Come in, Skip. Come in, *please*. This is urgent!"

"What is it?"

"Meet me out front!"

"Why?"

"Swerdlow just brought a package home."

"FRANKIE, I don't know. Maybe it *is* just a package."

"Mario, the last time we saw him he was getting into the backseat of a car that belonged to the Dark Hand Gang, right?"

"You made that up."

"Then the next time we see him he has a package."

"It was days apart!"

"The thing is, it could have loot in it. Or a bomb. Or secret plans. All we have to do is find out, get the info to the FBI, and we'll be heroes, right?"

"I suppose."

"And see, Mr. Swerdlow would have to move out, right?"

"Yeah . . ."

"Which is the first part of our plot, isn't it? Skipper, somebody has been listening to our prayers."

"I'm not going into his room again."

"Got it!"

"Got what?"

"Wheat Chips presents Chet Barker, the masked super spy, along with his always faithful and loyal sidekick, Skipper O'Malley. The world thinks they're just Frankie and Mario. But the criminal underworld fears them as Chet Barker and Skipper O'Malley, two gallant and resourceful boys who struggle increasingly against the sinister forces of evil. Tonight, the Adventure of the Apple Dumpling!"

"HEY, MA . . ."

"What is it? Oh, hello, Mario. How are you? How's your mother?"

"She's working."

"You say hello to her for me, will you? I never get to see her anymore."

"I don't get to see her much either, Mrs. Wattleson."

"What is it, Frankie?"

"Mom, are there any more apple dumplings left?"

"A couple. Why?"

"Could I bring one to Mr. Swerdlow?"

"Well . . . what makes you think of that?"

"He just came home. And I said hello, and he said hello. But remember that time Mario and I were looking at the skeleton in his closet?"

"Yes, and I told you—"

"I think he's still mad at us. So, I thought if we could bring him one of those dumplings and say we're sorry again—"

"Oh. That *is* a nice thought. I bet that was Mario's idea."

"Oh, no, Mrs. Wattleson. It's Frankie's."

"Well, it's nice. Frankie, I like it when you're considerate of other people. Here, take this one. It's the best."

"OKAY, SKIPPER, we've got the hypnotic pill."

"Where?"

"The dumpling, dummy!"

"What'll it do?"

"It'll cloud the mind of that murdering polecat and make him reveal the mysterious contents of the package. Now all we have to do is parachute down into his Nazi bunker. It's a thousand feet underground. You say, 'I'm right with you, Chet.' "

"I'm right with you, Chet."

"We check our disguises. I'm dressed like an old cook. You're disguised as a husky."

"A what?"

"A dog."

"No one would believe that!"

"A pet ape, then."

"Can't I just be Skipper?"

"Okay, Skipper, you're dressed as my butler. I say, 'Check your miniature six-shooter, Skip.' You say, 'Quite.' "

"Why do I say 'Quite'?"

"It's England, like on 'Sherlock Holmes.' That's the way they do it."

"I don't think there are any Nazi bunkers in England."

"Well, anyway, Skipper, we march boldly up the steps, hearts pounding."

"I thought you said it was down."

"Mario, for God's sake! What's the difference? It's

an adventure! I say, 'Skip, your legs are shaking.'
You say, 'I'm nervous about that bounder.' "

"I'm nervous about that bounder."

"We slip silently past the guards by going into the
bush. Sometimes it's up as well as down. A maze.
No one notices who we are. I whisper, 'This is it.'
You say, 'I'm a scared, Chet.' "

"It's true, Frankie."

"I say, 'Won't be long.' I knock."

"Yes? Who's there?"

"It's me, Mr. Swerdlow. Frankie."

"What do you want?"

"My mother sent something up for you."

"Just a minute. . . ."

"He's hiding it."

"How do you know?"

"When you knock on a criminal's door, they *always* hide things."

"Yes, Frankie. What is it?"

"My mother wanted you to have this apple dumpling."

"Oh! Well, that's very nice of her."

"I better bring it in."

"That's not necess—"

"Right here?"

"Fine. Tell your mother thank you."

"Say, Mr. Swerdlow, I see you got yourself a
package. . . ."

"Why, yes, I did. . . ."

"You going to eat that dumpling?"

"As soon as I finish my studying. Be my reward. Thanks a lot, boys."

"Was that a mail package?"

"Frankie, I have an exam tomorrow."

"We could unwrap it for you."

"Okay, boys, time to go."

"It would give you more time—"

"Frankie—"

"See you later, Mr. Swerdlow."

"Fine."

"Now what?"

"Skipper, we have no choice. We're going to have to get Miss Gomez to come here."

"How you going to do that, Chet?"

"Skipper, understand that our ultimate purpose is the extermination of the most rascally and dangerous criminal in the world! A traitor to the United States! A fiend who has cost the lives of thousands of our countrymen! I am speaking of the one known as . . ."

"Mr. Swerdlow."

"You got it, Skipper."

"Wow."

"But first . . ."

"What?"

"I think 'Buck Rodgers' is on."

"'Buck Rodgers is back on the air. Buck and Wilma and all their fascinating friends and mys—

terious enemies in the superscientific twenty-
fifth century.''

''This program is brought to you by the makers
of Popsicle, Fudgsicle, and Creamsicle, those
delicious frozen confections on a stick. Boy, do
they taste good and wholesome and nourishing,
made fresh every day of the finest ingredients,
the biggest five cents' worth anywhere!''

''And now for Buck Rodgers and his thrilling
adventures five hundred years in the future.

''As you probably know, Buck was born right
here in our own times, in this twentieth century, and the story of how he got started on his
amazing adventures so far in the future is
mighty interesting. But instead of telling you
about it, let's turn the dial that'll project us
ahead in time and find out all about it that way.

''Now, the capital of twenty-fifth-century
America is Niagara, and there it is that Doctor
Huer, the great scientist, has his marvelous
laboratory.

''In one room of it he's working on a strange-
looking device that sends a peculiar green
light down on a human figure lying on a table
before him. Shall we join him there? Okay,
then, here we go, five hundred years into the
future. . . .''

"Episode 10"

"ALL RIGHT, class, let's take out our *On the Long Road* readers. I believe we're up to page two-eighty. Yes, Ronald?"

"Miss Gomez, I left my book home."

"Move over to Joel's desk. You can read along with him. And Ronald, why don't you start reading—page two-eighty—the section entitled 'In the Observatory.' This should be very interesting, class."

"Now?"

"Yes, Ronald, now."

"Okay. Where it says, 'Uncle Jack'?"

"Exactly."

" 'Un-cle-Jack-led-the-way-in-to-the-huge-dome-room-of-the-ob-ser-va-tor-y-period-there-comma-

stand-ing-be-neath-the-great-op-en-slit-through-
which-the-star-ry-sky-could-be-seen-comma-was-
the-tel-es-cope-with-its-great-mir-ror-period-so-
large-and—' "

"Ronald, try not to stress every syllable equally.
It's *un*-cle. Not *un-cle*. Start again at 'So large.' "

"Now?"

"Yes, now."

" 'So-large-and-so-ov-er-pow-er-ing-did-it-seem-
to-Bob-that-he-just-looked-at-it-and-won-dered-
period-sev-e-ral-as-tron—' "

"Ronald, excuse me. You don't need to *read* the
punctuation. Just include it naturally in your reading. Comma, brief pause. Period, longer pause.
New paragraph, even longer pause. Continue,
please. And try to read with some expression."

"Okay. 'Sev-e-ral-as-tron-o-mers-were-work-ing-
there-as-they-work-each-night-in-ob-serv-a-tor-ies-
all-ov-er-the-world-and-Un-cle-Jack-sig . . . sig . . . ' "

" 'Signaled.' "

" 'Sig-naled-Bob-to-be-qui-et.' "

"Yes, Ronald, go on."

"I'm pausing."

"Not such a long pause. Go on."

" 'Bob-spent-a-won-der-ful-half-hour-in-that-
bus-y-qui-et-place-just-be-fore-it-was-time-for-him-
to-leave-Un-cle-Jack-whis-pered-"Fol-low-me"-
and-Bob-found-him-self-be-fore-one-of-the-great-
tel-es-copes-he-was-act-u-al-ly-look-ing-at-the-

stars - through - a - real - tel - es - cope - ex - cit - ed - and -
hap-py-he-said-"good-night"-and-"thank-you"-to-
Un-cle-Jack.' "

"Yes, Franklin? What is it?"

"Do you think this Bob saw any spaceships, or
maybe even mysterious enemies?"

"I don't understand."

"You know, people from the twenty-fifth century.
Last night on 'Buck Rodgers'—"

"Class! That's enough, Franklin."

"Well, Miss Gomez, see, if Doctor Huer had invented that telescope he—"

"Franklin, once again you will stay after school."

"*PSST* . . . Frankie . . ."

"Keep your voice down, Skipper. We're under
surveillance."

"You do that on purpose?"

"Sure."

"Why?"

"Tell you later."

"FRANKLIN WATTLESON . . ."

"Yes, Miss Gomez."

"Do you know how very close I am to giving up?"

"Two inches."

"What did I tell you last time, Franklin?"

"You gave me your number and said I should tell
my parents to call."

"And?"

"They ran out of nickels."

"I don't believe that. Well, then . . . I guess I'm really going to have to visit your parents at your home."

"Yeah. . . ."

"That would be quite the humiliation, wouldn't it?"

"Be okay with me."

"You would *not* mind?"

"Nope."

"I'm not so sure I believe that either. I suggest you read your reader."

"Okay."

"Franklin?"

"Yes, Miss Gomez."

"Did you *want* to be kept in this afternoon?"

"Miss Gomez, you don't shoot a man who gives his whole life to doing good for other people."

"Franklin, there are times I simply do not understand you."

"GREAT SCOTT!"

"What's the matter, Franklin?"

"Well, you told me to read this, and I was. Only, then I started thinking about something."

"What?"

"I don't want to say."

"Why?"

"You might get angry again."

"I promise I won't. Now, go on. What is it that made you excited?"

"See, I was just thinking how nifty it would be if that boy Bob and his uncle Jack might have seen something really great when they were looking through that telescope. Like, maybe Bob has radio vision—"

"What's radio vision?"

"Don't you know?"

"Franklin, asking questions is the way intelligent people become educated."

"Oh. Well, radio vision is what the Silver Fox has. Lets him see behind or into things. Except cotton. For some reason he can't see through—"

"That's enough, Franklin."

"But I thought you wanted to become—"

"Enough!"

"Yes, Miss Gomez."

"Franklin?"

"Yes, Miss Gomez."

"Don't you like *anything* about school?"

"I like you."

"Thank you. And I like you too, Franklin. But I'm not sure our liking each other is what school is about. Don't you care about your work?"

"You want the truth?"

"You should always tell the truth."

"School's boring."

"Why?"

"It's the same every day. On radio it's—"

"Franklin, I've made up my mind: I *will* make a visit to your home."

"Oh, great!"

"You don't mean that."

"I do. When you coming?"

"That will be for me to decide."

"Will it be soon?"

"Yes, soon."

"Episode 11"

"OKAY, YOU SET?"

"Yeah."

"Here goes. Corn Bits—the crunchy cereal that made farmers famous—presents Chet Barker, the masked and brilliant but resourceful super GI-spy with his faithful but also brilliant scientific sidekick, Skipper O'Malley. Most folks think they're only kids."

"The evil underworld knows better."

"Chet Barker fights evil where 'ere he finds it—"

"No matter how under- or overhanded—"

"In a troubled, confused, mixed-up, twisted, and also puzzled world. This morning—the Adventure of Doctor Swerdlow's Secret Surprise."

"Frankie, you really sure he's out?"

"It's Saturday. Saturday mornings he always goes out."

"That's what you said last time."

"Mario, I just saw him walk down the street. Anyway, we're not going into his closet. Just his room to see about that package."

"Why?"

"To find out what's inside it."

"Maybe there's nothing."

"Packages always have something in them."

"But even if it does, how's that going to help us?"

"Mario, have you ever, even once, ever heard of an evil scientist who had a package that didn't have evidence in it?"

"But that's *radio*, and this—"

"Skipper, there are moments I suspect you'd be happier finding someone else to kick along the side of."

"Frankie, I'm just saying—"

"The thing is, Skipper, Miss Gomez will be visiting soon. So we have to find a way to get rid of Mr. Swerdlow fast. That package might be it."

"Maybe it's just his laundry. Socks. Or underpants. Yeah, what if it's his underpants?"

"Have you ever heard about underpants on radio, ever?"

"Well, no . . ."

"Okay, then. Now, today, as we discover our

young heroes, it's a dark, dreary, dull, dumb, drizzling December day."

"That's a lot of *D* words."

"Come on, Mario! I say, 'Skipper, if we fail tonight, it will be the end of us all. If we are successful, our country will be saved.' You say, 'Gosh.' "

"Gosh."

"Okay, we parachute down from a B-17. We land. No one sees us. I say, 'The coast is clear. Easy does it.' You say, 'I'm right behind you, Chet.' "

"I'm right behind you, Chet."

"Sneaking through the brush, we approach the tunnel. You say, 'Hope there ain't no bats, Chet.' "

"Hope there ain't no bats, Chet."

"I say, 'Nothing to worry about, Skipper. We've got our Atomic Radio Beeper with its Mobile Death Stinger Power Badge. It'll take care of any bats. You ought to know, Skip—you invented all that stuff yourself.' You say, 'Phew.' "

"Phew."

"The door opens. Hinges creak. Our hearts start going *thuda-thuda-thuda*. Sweat drips. I say, 'This is it, Skipper.' You say, 'I'm ready.' "

"I'm ready."

"Then I say, 'Look there!' And you say, 'What the—?' "

"Just 'What the—?' "

"You know!"

"Okay. What the—?"

"They've got six thousand ancient Aztecs waiting

for us. But by switching on your patented Invisibility Cloaks, we're able to creep right through them."

"I'm really nervous, Frankie."

"It'll be fine, Skipper."

"I'm just scared—that's all."

"Okay. We go on faster. Open the door. Flip on the lights. Look! There's the package on the table."

"Maybe I should go—"

"We step closer. . . ."

"Frankie, will you hurry! I don't want to get caught."

"Chet Barker opens the package."

"What is it? What's the matter? What's there?"

"Look!"

"What?"

"Look."

"Holy moley. A skull! I'm going home."

"Me too."

"MARIO! Let me in."

"Can't. My mother said I had to stay in while she's shopping."

"When she coming back?"

"Couple of hours."

"We have to talk."

"Frankie, if my mother knew I was finding skulls—"

"Mario, do you know what that skull means?"

"Somebody died."

"It's probably a plot to destroy America."

"Nothing to do with me."

"Some patriotic sidekick you are."

"I'm going to resign."

"Sidekicks can't resign."

"Sure, they can. Just because you're always the boss doesn't mean I have to do everything you say. I could join a union. A sidekick union. Yeah. I could go on a sidekick strike."

"Mario, cross my heart and hope to die. I just want to talk."

"Promise? No fins?"

"No fins."

"Swear on your mother?"

"On my mother."

"On your mother's mother?"

"My mother's mother."

"Okay. But not in here. And just for a short time. I'll meet you out front."

"MARIO, Mr. Swerdlow having a skull on his table proves that he's evil."

"I don't care. I don't want anything to do with him."

"Not even if it means saving the world?"

"No."

"Why?"

"My mother would get too upset."

"Mario, why do you have to worry about your mother so much?"

"You have a mother and a father and a brother, right?"

"Yeah."

"And an uncle."

"Well, I suppose, except I don't think anyone around here wants to see him except me."

"Well, all I've got is a mother."

"I know that, Mario, but, the thing is, we'd be heroes. Real ones."

"You always say that, but all that happens is we get into trouble."

"Mario, you can't be a hero unless you get into trouble first."

"No one's going to believe us."

"Same difference: people never believe in heroes. Not at first. It's kind of a rule. So heroes go against all odds and obstacles, battling the forces of evil with skill and cunning until the truth is revealed to those who are weak but still desperately want some unvarnished justice."

"Frankie?"

"What?"

"Do you believe all that stuff you say?"

"What stuff?"

"Your radio stuff. Can't you ever talk regular?"

"Heroes don't talk regular."

"But Frankie, Mr. Swerdlow is *real*. That skull was real. I mean, what do you think he does with it? Really."

"Uses it to mix poisons he's going to drop into the city's water system. That way he gets everyone into his power. And the Nazis take over. So the free world is in more danger than ever before."

"Frankie, be serious! The Nazis are just about beaten!"

"Don't worry. If there are heroes, then there have to be enemies. And every man, woman, and child in the free world is waiting for us—you and me— Chet Barker and his pal Skipper—to find them."

"Frankie, kids—*real* kids—can't do anything."

"Sure they can!"

"Name one thing kids can do. Go on. I dare you. Double dare you. Triple!"

"Okay. What do you see over there?"

"On the street?"

"Yeah. What do you see?"

"The street. Houses. Windows. Doors. And people. Cars. And the mailman coming."

"Naw. That's the way grown-ups see. You want to know what I can see?"

"What?"

"One of those cars is a disguised rocket car. And behind that window—with the service star—there's a genius inventor. And that person walking there has a secret identity. And it could be the mailman is really a G-man, or even Doctor Oddball, and in his bag he's got an Instant Radio Double Relay Spy Noticer."

"You don't *know* any of that."

"So what? Everything would be better that way, wouldn't it?"

"I suppose."

"Well, *that's* what kids can do. Mario, look, what I'm saying—about Mr. Swerdlow—is that if it turns out to be true and you did nothing, you'd hate yourself. Wouldn't you? Admit it."

"Well . . ."

"People would be saying, 'There goes Mario Calvino, who could have saved the world but didn't want to.' So instead, no one's alive because you turned soft. That what you want all those dead people saying? Or would you rather have them say, 'Ta-da! Here comes Mario Calvino. He was only a kid, but he saw the truth and, against all odds, saved us.' Your ma would be so proud of you, wouldn't she? Admit it."

"I know, but—"

"Mario, we can do it!"

"Well, maybe. But only if you don't tell my mother till *after* we save the world."

"Wattleson?"

"Yes, sir."

"Here's your morning mail, kiddo."

"Thanks. . . . Great Scott, Skipper! A letter from Miss Gomez."

"For you?"

"My parents."

"Think it's bad news?"

"Hope so."

"Boy, if she wrote my mother . . ."

"When did you say your mother's coming home?"

"Another hour."

"Skipper, when you intercept a secret message—in an envelope—there's only one thing to do: steam it open."

"Frankie . . ."

"Don't worry, Skipper. *The Sky King Junior Spy Manual* explains it all."

"GEE, I never thought steaming really worked."

"Sky King doesn't lie. The letter open, Chet Barker reads it quickly. Oh, swell!"

"What's it say?"

" 'Dear Mr. and Mrs. Wattleson: As you may know, I am Franklin's sixth grade teacher at Public School Number Eight. While he is a pleasant child and, in his way, harmless, I am afraid that there have been serious problems regarding both his behavior and performance in school this term. I am truly concerned about him. I feel we must sit down and talk. May I call upon you both at your home this coming Thursday evening at seven? Sincerely, Esmeralda Gomez.' "

"Frankie, you are in big trouble."

"No, I'm not. She is."

"What do you mean?"

"Mario, don't you get *anything*? See, she thinks I'm pleasant and *harmless*. That's just what I wanted her to think. The mask worked. She doesn't know my secret identity. Crash of thunder. Burst of lightning. Da-dum! This is a job for—Chet Barker!"

"MA . . ."

"Mmm . . ."

"I forgot to tell you something."

"What's that?"

"At school yesterday, my teacher—Miss Gomez —said to tell our parents that there's a special meeting at school Thursday evening. All parents *have* to attend."

"What kind of meeting?"

"I just said. For parents."

"I was asking you why."

"They want to draft all sixth graders into the navy."

"*What?*"

"It's for a new fleet of midget submarines. Grown-ups can't fit into them. So they have to use kids."

"Frankie, you give me a headache. Just tell me what it is."

"It's about what class I'm supposed to be in next year."

"They never used to hold such meetings."

"It's part of the war effort. Saves paper."

"When is it?"

"Next Thursday. Seven o'clock. And if all the parents come, every kid in the class gets a Popsicle, Fudgsicle, or Creamsicle, those delicious frozen confections on a stick."

"A Fudgsicle?"

"Well, they do taste good and wholesome and nourishing. And they're made fresh every day of the finest ingredients. The biggest five cents' worth anywhere! So Pop has to go too."

"I think Mr. Giorgi needs him. He'll be working."

"Will you go?"

"I suppose."

"Okay. I'll tell Miss Gomez yes."

"SAY, SKIPPER, things are really starting to fall into place. You say, 'Let's hear the scoop.'"

"Let's hear the scoop."

"Skipper, I've devised a plan that gets my parents out of the house at the precise moment Miss Gomez visits."

"How'd you do that?"

"Told them there was an urgent meeting at school for parents."

"Who's going to be at your house, then?"

"Tom."

"You going to tell him?"

"Skipper, that's the whole point. It goes this way: My parents are going to be out. Meanwhile, back at the homestead, the young and pretty Miss Esmeralda Gomez, lovely daughter of a wealthy rancher, comes to the door. It's night. A quick, tropic twilight slides its way over the city. Miss Gomez knocks on the door. *Tap, tap.* Sound echoes through the old mansion. Mice scurry away. The only one who can answer is handsome young Tom, recently wounded in glorious battle. Reluctantly but painfully, he hobbles to the door. He opens it. The hinges creak. To his surprise it's Miss Gomez, whom he forgets to recognize as the lovely daughter of a wealthy rancher. Well, Skipper, these two healthy young people look at each other. They stare into each other's eyes. For the moment Tom's pain is forgotten. Miss Gomez loses her mind too. Their hearts melt. Zing!"

"Zing *what*?"

"Skipper, it's a story as old as the world. And just as new. They fall in love."

"Wow. . . ."

"Sure. And get married. That's the way it happens."

"Wait a minute. You're always saying Tom just stays in his room and won't see anyone. What if he won't go to the door?"

"He will."

"How come?"

"I'll figure something."

"Or . . . yeah, what if it's Mr. Swerdlow who answers the door and Miss Gomez falls in love with *him*?"

"Skipper, did you ever, ever once hear of a beautiful woman who fell in love with an evil scientist?"

"Frankie, she doesn't know he's evil! Admit it. You didn't think of that."

"Okay, we'll have to make sure Doc Swerdlow is already gone."

"How we going to do that?"

"I'll think of something. Anyway, with him gone, it'll make it easier for the young married couple to move into that room."

"Think they'll get married that fast?"

"Before the end of the term."

"What about getting the radio for yourself?"

"Skipper, Chet Barker expects no reward but the love of his grateful countrymen."

"None?"

"Well, a radio would be nice."

⚡

"Conklin's Corn Cracks presents the 'Adventures of the Silver Fox'!

"By day Jim Buck drives a taxi through the city streets. By night he dons the cape and mask of the Silver Fox. With his devoted companion, Benny O'Toole, crackerjack schoolboy mechanic, he tracks down and brings to justice those public enemies who might otherwise outrun the reaches of the law!

"In just a minute we'll begin today's adventure."

"Say, boys and girls, do you know what it is to get up in the morning feeling stiff and tired, with not much get up and go? Of course you do. It happens to us all. But I know you want to get to school alert, full of vigor and vim, so you can be a tip–top student! Well, kids, Conklin's Corn Cracks will give you all the energy you need and then some. Smothered with bits of fresh fruit, showered with good–for–you wholesome milk, a breakfast of Conklin's Corn Cracks will start you off right. And it tastes so super-delicious too, with a rich corn taste that you'll just love. So tell your mom and dad you want to do the very best you can, and a breakfast of Conklin's Corn Cracks will help you do just that. Tomorrow morning, then, start your day the Conklin's Corn Cracks way!

"And now, for today's story, which is called Can the Dead Talk?"

"It is night, and the great city is deserted. But a sinister hooded figure is moving backward along the streets and alleys. In his hands he's holding a spool, and from it he's carefully playing out a thin wire and laying it carefully against the shadows."

"Just a few more blocks and this will be set, and then, Mr. Clayton Adams . . ."

"The hooded figure reaches his destination but not the end of his mission. Still trailing the wire, he silently makes his way up the fire escape. Just outside the window of Apartment Five–C, he sets down a tiny but powerful speaker and carefully fastens his wire to it. When he is certain all the proper connections have been made, he chuckles to himself."

''Okay, Mr. Clayton Adams, let's see how you deal with strange voices coming from nowhere.''

''Laughing silently, the hooded figure scurries away as unnoticed as when he came.

''It's two days later, and we're in the secret garage beneath the city apartment where Jim Buck lives. He's with his youthful assistant, Benny O'Toole, who not only serves as his crackerjack mechanic, but is the one person who knows the true identity of the Silver Fox.''

''You're looking worried, Jim.''

''I am, Benny. My friend Clayton Adams died yesterday.''

''The ace newspaper reporter?''

''That's him. He was hot on the heels of a dangerous spy ring. The newspapers say he committed suicide, driven insane by strange voices.''

''Yeah. I read about that. Rotten bad.''

''But committing suicide is not the kind of thing Clayton would do.''

''It sure seems odd. Strange voices . . .''

''Yes, I suspect some diabolically clever men are behind this.''

''Sounds like work for the Silver Fox.''

''That's just what I thought. Is the Rocket Motorcycle ready?''

''Sure as shamrocks, boss. Where you headed?''

''I've got a hunch that might just yield something.''

''A clue?''

''Maybe. It seems that shortly before Clayton

died he sent a letter to the district attorney.
At least that's what his mother said. The DA
never got it."

"Sounds suspicious."

"Yes, I think I'll check it out."

"Good luck!"

"Benny steps back and throws a switch. A secret door swings open. Jim Buck, now garbed in
the distinctive silver jacket and mask of the
Silver Fox, leaps upon the white Rocket Motorcycle. A push of a button and its motors are acti-
vated. Then, with a silent roar, the Rocket
Motorcycle leaps up a ramp and hurtles onto the
dark streets of the great city. The Silver Fox
is on the scent!"

"Episode 12"

"MARIO!"

"What?"

"I figured a way to get rid of Mr. Swerdlow."

"How?"

"The Atomic Radio Remote Relay!"

"I don't get it."

"Skipper, with your scientific genius, along with my courage and daring, there's nothing we can't do. You say, 'Easy as aces, Chet.' "

"Easy as aces, Chet. Just say it, Frankie."

"Skipper, what we're going to do is hide that Atomic Radio Remote Relay speaker in Mr. Swerdlow's skull."

"His *head*?"

"The one in that package. Then we'll run the wire

down to my basement place. When he's in his room, we make strange, ghostlike noises. He'll believe the room is haunted. Crooks are always superstitious. By gumption, Skipper, he'll be gone in nothing flat."

"No."

"What do you mean, no?"

"I'm not going into his room again."

"Mario, this is my best idea, ever!"

"We always get caught."

"Mario, if kids like us—fun-loving, loyal Americans—don't fight the sinister hand of crime and subversion when 'ere it rears its ugly head, who's going to do it?"

"Not me."

"Make a deal. . . . If you help me with this, I'll give you my Silver Fox Decoder Badge *and* my Captain Midnight Ovaltine Mug."

"No."

"What about if I threw in my Lone Ranger Emergency Whistle Ring?"

"Well . . ."

"Honest."

"Decoder Badge, Ovaltine Mug, and Whistle Ring?"

"Once we get the speaker into the skull."

"Is the other end going to be in your house or mine?"

"Mine. In the basement."

"And you'll really give me that stuff?"

"I'll even add my *Green Llama Junior G-man Manual*."

"Okay."

"I hear you, Skipper. I hear you loud and clear. Come on."

"AS WE join our friends, it's long past midnight. Chet Barker and his faithful sidekick, Skipper, have just flown over from England. Under cover of darkness they parachute down from a B-17. The air is fierce. Leaves are frozen, and clouds have thickened. The moon is the color of fear. An owl hoots. You say, 'Chet, I've snuck up ahead to see if the coast is clear. It is.' "

"Chet, I've snuck up ahead to see if the coast is clear. It is."

"Awful decent of you, the way you do things on your own, Skipper. Now, first thing we better do is get the Atomic Relay Remote Radio speaker into Doc Swerdlow's skull. You set?"

"We're going to get caught, Frankie. I know we are. I *feel* it."

"It's Sunday, and Sunday mornings he visits his grandfather in a nursing home."

"Wish I had a grandfather to visit."

"Okay, Skipper, I'll take the lead. You say, 'Right behind you, Chet.' "

"Right behind you, Chet."

"I say, 'Don't make a sound.' You say, 'I won't.' Go on, say it."

"But if I say 'I won't,' I am making a sound."

"Forget it. Okay, we go up the steps. Someone takes a shot at us. *Ping!* Missed me. Miss you, Skipper?"

"No. It creased my skull. I can't go on."

"Mario, you promised! Okay, we go up a hundred hard stone steps. Now we're outside the Public Enemies' High Command bunker. We lay low, making sure no one's around. Breathing hard, I say, 'Skipper, if I don't get out of this alive, say hello to Bette for me.' "

"She the one who's doing the report on Mexico in class?"

"Yeah."

"Didn't know you liked her."

"I don't. I'm just saying it. Okay. I peek out. I see the coast is clear. We approach the door. Suddenly, seventeen storm troopers leap forward in a deadly ambush. Oh-oh, Skipper, we're in trouble. We fall back, our guns blazing. *Ping! Pow! Slam!* Machine guns spray the air! Quick. The Automatic Ambush Breaker!"

"*Buzz! Buzz!*"

"Great going, Skipper. You got them all. Okay, I open the trapdoor. The hinges creak. I step inside. *Step, step.* Turn on the hidden button. *Click!* You follow."

"Where's the skull?"

"I don't know. Look under his pillow."

"Isn't there. Try the closet."

"Yeah."

"Oh, wow."

"See, he fixed the skull on top of the rest of the bones. Must be a shrine."

"Isn't that skull a little small for the rest of it?"

"He probably shrank it."

"How'd he do that?"

"You can get special skull shrink mixes. Slide the chair over."

"Frankie, you know what? I think the skull is too small for the speaker."

"Shhh! Look out!"

"Oh, God, Frankie! You knocked the whole skeleton down! It's broken! Now what are we going to do?"

"Come on. We have to put it back together."

"He's going to come back, Frankie. I know he is!"

"No, he isn't. And it's not broken. Just a couple of pieces fell off. The rest is attached with wires. Come on, put the speaker down and help me put this up again."

"I don't want to touch it."

"Mario, if we leave it like this, he'll know we came in for sure. Come on!"

"It's heavy."

"Mario, lift some more!"

"I'm trying!"

"Look out for the ribs."

"Frankie, it kicked me!"

"Higher!"

"I hate this!"

"More!"

"It's slipping!"

"Almost! Okay. There."

"Frankie?"

"What?"

"I'm going to be sick."

"Hold it till you get back home."

"But what about those two pieces? Where do they come from?"

"This one could be part of an arm. Or a rib. I'll slide it in here."

"Frankie, a person wouldn't have a bone going from one side of his chest to the other side—right through the lungs. Makes it look like an arrow."

"What about here?"

"That's okay. Do something with the other one."

"This all right?"

"Frankie, no one has fingers two feet long!"

"Okay. There."

"That's better. Now let's get out of here."

"Wait! The speaker. Where we going to put it?"

"There?"

"Mario, a ghost wouldn't be caught dead in a dirty clothes hamper. I know. Under his bed. Great. Now we run the wire out the window. See if it reaches down enough."

"It does."

"Okay, Skipper, *now* let's get out of here."

"MARIO! Here comes the wire down the coal chute. Grab it."

"What happens if you get a coal delivery?"

"They don't deliver Sundays."

"Everything's filthy with coal dust. My mother doesn't want me to get dirty Sundays."

"Pretend it's Monday. Now take the wire and run it over to the sender."

"Got it."

"YOU GET IT hooked up yet?"

"I think so. Where we going to plug it in?"

"Over there."

"Go on."

"Here goes, Skipper. Okay. All plugged in. Is it on?"

"It's humming."

"That mean it's working?"

"Can't tell until we try."

"Have to wait for Mr. Swerdlow to come back."

"When's that going to be?"

"Should be before lunch. Skipper, I'm telling you, that evil genius will be out of that room so fast . . . You see, Skipper, all it takes is a little American know-how. The kind of thinking that our enemies—who forever despise our way of life—can never seem to get right."

"Hope we don't blow a fuse."

"Let's go sit out on the stoop and wait for him."

"HELLO, BOYS."

"Oh, hi, Mr. Swerdlow."

"Nice day, isn't it?"

"You bet. Hey, Mr. Swerdlow, how's your grand-father?"

"Fine, thank you."

"You going to do any operating this morning?"

"Not today, Frankie. I've got exams to study for. See you fellows later."

"See you."

"YOU READY?"

"I'm really nervous."

"Mario, if we fail, it will be the end of us all. If we're successful, we'll be saved from defeat."

"Cut it out, Frankie. Just makes me more scared."

"Okay, here we go. Ta-dum! Chet Barker, Master Spy!"

"Da-dum, da-dum!"

"Shredded Bran Chips brings you another thrill-ing adventure with Chet Barker, Master Spy! Chet Barker, ruthless, clear-eyed, fearless, and smartly dressed! Chet Barker, thundering out of the dim past in a constant search for his own true identity! Chet Barker, fighting hand to hand for what's im-portant on the land!"

"On the sea!"

"And in the air! Da-dum! With his faithful side-kick, Skipper O'Malley—known for his nervous but crackerjack scientific mind—Chet Barker *believes* in the American way!"

"Da-dum!"

"And now for today's adventure, The Skull Speaks! As we join them, Chet and Skipper are kneeling beside their Atomic Radio Relay Radio Station somewhere deep beneath the bowls of the earth. Night, like a black blotter, sucks up their spit, leaving their mouths dry with a crust of fear! As we join them, Chet turns and whispers, 'Skipper, this is it. The moment we've all been waiting for.' You say—"

"Frankie, I really don't think we should do this."

"Come on, Mario! No fair going back. I gave you all that stuff. Now, soon as you turn the ARSR on, make the wind noises."

"Three *R*'s. Atomic Radio Relay Radio Station. You never get it right."

"Doesn't matter."

"It does!"

"Anyway, I'll do deathly howls. And the words."

"Frankie, maybe he's not in his room."

"We just saw him go up, didn't we?"

"He could be in the bathroom."

"Not going to stay forever."

"If he were reading one of those huge medical books, he might. Did you see how big they were?"

"Mario!"

"Okay. It's on."

"Start. . . ."

"Wooooooosh. . . . Wooooooosh. . . ."

"Oooooooooo! Oooooooooo! Oooooooooo!"

"Wooooooosh. . . ."

"Who knows the awful things that evil scientists do? The skeleton knows! Ha-ha-ha-ha-ha!"

"Wooooooosh. . . ."

"Oooooooooo! Oooooooooo! Oooooooooo!"

"Wooooooosh. . . ."

"Yes, this is the voice of your skeleton speaking from beyond the grave."

"Wooooooosh. . . ."

"Yes! This is an evil place! A haunted place. Give it up! Be gone. Be gone. Ha-ha-ha-ha-ha. The skeleton knows! Okay. Turn it off."

"Think it worked?"

"Skipper, at this very moment that varmint is shaking in his boots."

"He doesn't wear boots."

"His shoes, then."

"Just hope he doesn't figure it out."

"They never do."

"He might."

"Skipper, I'm a telling you, once a man like that gets afeared, there is nothing on earth a going to stop him from— Oh, hi, Mr. Swerdlow. You looking for something?"

"I thought so."

"What?"

"Is this your idea of a joke, Frankie?"

"What's that?"

"This speaker was under my bed."

"It was?"

"And the wires ran out the window right down to this basement."

"They did?"

"And you've got the rest of the apparatus, I see. Don't you kids have the slightest regard for privacy? How many times have I told you, *Keep out of my room!*"

"Just an experiment."

"Experiment?"

"Well, Mario here is a genius like Thomas Edison, and when he invented the Remote Atomic Radio Relay—"

"Frankie, I'm sick of your nonsense. Absolutely fed up. Now get up out of there! We're going right to your parents. Come on—move!"

"MR. WATTLESON?"

"Oh, hi, Mr. Swerdlow. How you doing? What's up?"

"Mr. Wattleson, I'm sorry to disturb you on a Sunday, but Frankie and his pal were in my room again."

"Oh, Lord. . . ."

"And this time, Mr. Wattleson, they went so far as to place a speaker under my bed and begin spouting gibberish."

"Frankie! How many times have I told you! Keep out of there!"

"We were chasing a rattlesnake—"

"A rattlesnake!"

"Mr. Wattleson, when I rent a room, I have a right to expect privacy. I keep my valuables there. My books. My—"

"Mr. Swerdlow, I promise. He'll be severely punished. You have my word. It won't happen again. And I'll tell you what: I'll buy you a lock. A Yale lock."

"Mr. Wattleson, I'm afraid there have been too many promises. Look, there are just two days left before the end of the month. I'm all paid up, and my exams will be over Tuesday. I think I'll just pack up and leave. I'm sorry. I must have privacy. This isn't working."

"Mr. Swerdlow—"

"I'm sorry, Mr. Wattleson. You and your wife and your older son have been very pleasant. I've no complaints on that score. But these boys. When I get home on Tuesday afternoon, shortly after five, I'll be packing up."

"Mr. Swerdlow—"

"Please tell your wife. Good afternoon."

"Mario, get out of here, fast!"

"Yes, Mr. Wattleson."

"And don't come around here again! You hear me? Beat it! Amscray!"

"Yes, sir."

"As for you . . ."

"Pop, honest, Mr. Swerdlow is really evil."

"*What?*"

"A public enemy."

"What are you, some kind of nut or something?"

"It's true!"

"That's ten bucks a week we're losing! Where do you think it's going to come from now?"

"Pop, the fate of the entire universe depended on it!"

"Let me tell you something, Frankie. When your mother comes home from church, we're going to figure out a punishment you ain't never going to forget. You understand? *Never!* I've had it with your fate of the entire universe! Now get down into your room. Fast! And don't even think of coming out till I say you can!"

"But—"

"Move it!"

"HI, MA."

"Don't 'Hi, Ma' me, young man. Just listen to your father."

"Frankie, sit down. This is serious. A family meeting. Just you, me, and your mother."

"Isn't Tom in the family?"

"Frankie, for once in your life, don't give me any lip. Just listen!"

"Can I eat a bowl of cereal while you're talking?"

"Frankie . . ."

"Or drink a glass of Ovaltine?"

"Frankie, that was a terrible thing you did to Mr. Swerdlow."

"Ma, he appears harmless. Don't be fooled—"

"Frankie, he paid his rent. We needed that money."

"Pop, it was just ill-gotten gains, an affront to all true Americans."

"What did you say?"

"Never mind. You don't care."

"Now you listen to me, Frankie. We're not going to take this junk you dish out anymore. Once and for all, it's got to stop! First off, no radio! No Mario! No playing outside! No nothing. You go to school. You come home. You do your work. That's it!"

"Can I eat breakfast?"

"Yes, you can eat!"

"If Mr. Swerdlow really goes, will Tom get back into his old—"

"Get into the basement!"

"But, Pop . . ."

"Frankie, your father is really angry!"

"Go! Go!"

"For how long?"

"For fifty years! But first I want to hear it from you: no more nonsense, right?"

"Pop, okay, I promise! But can I say just one thing?"

"What?"

"Don't forget that meeting Thursday night."

"What's he talking about?"

"The very, very important, absolutely crucial, desperate, exciting meeting with Miss Gomez, my teacher."

"Get down there and stay there!"

"WHO'S KNOCKING?"

"It's me, Mario. Frankie. Let me in quick!"

"How come you're so dirty?"

"Climbed out through the coal chute."

"Why'd you do that?"

"My parents locked me in the basement as punishment. I have to stay there for the rest of my life. But guess what? Mr. Swerdlow's really moving out."

"Oh, wow."

"See. Told you kids could do things."

"Yeah, but if your parents tell my mother, she's going to kill me."

"Mario, you're always saying that, but—be honest—has she ever done it?"

"No."

"Well?"

"It only takes once."

"Don't worry—she's not going to kill you. Anyway, here's the Remote Atomic Radio Relay Radio and some more wire. We can keep running it from here back down to the basement."

"Is that why you came?"

"Don't want to miss any shows."

"Episode 13"

"COME IN, Skipper! Come in. This is urgent!"

"What is it?"

"Mr. Swerdlow's about to leave."

"So what?"

"He has to be watched!"

"Why?"

"To see if he reveals anything."

"You do it."

"I can't. I'm locked in this dungeon. It has to be you."

"I don't know how."

"Just sit on the stoop, and when he comes out, cloud his mind."

"Do what?"

"Cloud his mind. Like the Shadow does."

"Frankie, I don't know how to do that stuff."

"Mario, all you do is look at him and then laugh that special way. It's the laughing that does it. You know—ha-ha-ha-ha-ha."

"I don't feel like laughing."

"Skipper, we have to demonstrate forcefully to old and young alike that crime does not pay."

"Frankie, I'm no good at that!"

"Come on, Mario. *Try!* I'll be listening. And if you get it wrong, I'll call it to you up the coal chute."

"Promise?"

"Yeah, promise. Just hurry. I hear him. He's coming down the steps with the last of his stuff. Try it."

"Ha-ha-ha."

"No, it's ha-ha-ha-*ha-ha*."

"Ha-ha-ha-ha-ha."

"That's it. Now go on—do it. And Godspeed."

"AH, HI, Mr. Swerdlow."

"Oh, Mario, hello. Well, I'm all set to go. I suppose I should say good-bye. Where's your pal?"

"In the basement. He's not allowed out."

"Well, I'm sorry. . . ."

"Ha-ha-ha-ha."

"What?"

"Ha-ha-ha-ha."

"Ha-ha-ha-ha-*ha*!"

"Who said that?"

"Said what?"

"That other sound."

"I didn't hear anything."

"Mario, I'm going to give you some advice. Find yourself another buddy."

"WHAT HAPPENED?"

"Nothing."

"You know why?"

"No."

"Well, what did you say?"

"All them ha-ha's."

"Mario, I *told* you—it's supposed to be *five* ha's. Didn't you hear me? I was trying to cue you."

"I got confused."

"Mario, I don't understand. You're so good in math. You could get it right. Well, anyway, we got rid of him. That's the important thing. And Skipper, there's still a lot of work to be done."

"That's what worries me."

"Episode 14"

"HEY, FRANKIE, I thought you weren't allowed out."

"My father's working. My ma went to the market. I need some fresh air. Keep a lookout."

"Where's Tom?"

"In his room."

"When's Miss Gomez coming?"

"Thursday."

"Still think the plot will work?"

"Got rid of Mr. Swerdlow, didn't we?"

"I suppose."

"We'll do the rest."

"Hey, Frankie . . ."

"What?"

"There's an old guy across the street. He keeps staring at us."

"Where?"

"Over there. See him?"

"Yeah."

"How come he's watching us?"

"I don't know. Looks like a tramp."

"He's coming over."

"Probably wants a handout."

"I'm going upstairs."

"Mario . . ."

"Hey, kid. This number one fifty-two Willow Street?"

"Yeah."

"Can I ask you something?"

"I don't have any money."

"I wasn't looking for money. Just want to know if you live here."

"How come?"

"Well, I . . . What's your name?"

"Chet Barker."

"Well, Chet, sonny, you ever hear of a Mary Wattleson? Married. Couple of kids. She still live here?"

"What about her?"

"She around?"

"Well . . . sort of."

"Not inside, is she?"

"Well, no. . . ."

"Don't misunderstand. I don't want to see her or anything. Fact is, be better if she *wasn't* here. You see—you say your name is Chet?"

"Chet Barker."

"Well, you see, Chet, what it is, I'm this Mary Wattleson's brother."

"You *are?*"

"I know. She's a nice lady. And I probably don't look so great. But it's true. She's my sister. My kid sister. Oh, sure. . . . We go back a long ways. But I haven't seen her for a few years. You say she's out?"

"Yeah."

"She used to have a husband. Albert. Big guy. Strong feller. I introduced him to my sister. But her husband and me, we didn't get along too well. Used to call me a chiseler. Which I was, in a way. He around?"

"No, sir. He's working."

"Okay. Mind if I sit down? Take a load off. Thanks. But you say they still live here?"

"Yeah."

"She had a couple of kids. A boy and—"

"Two boys."

"Two boys. Right. Boys. They must be pretty old by now."

"One is a general in the army."

"Big shot, huh?"

"But he got wounded."

"You don't say? I'm telling you, people grow up. Change. They do. What about the other one?"

"Became a Secret Service man."

"Is that a fact? Amazing. . . ."

"Mister, if you're my . . . her brother, how come you don't know about her?"

"Well, I've been away awhile. Yup, been away."

"Then how come you don't want to see her?"

"Truth is, sonny, she'd get all upset if she saw me. I mean, you know, I might be an embarrassment. See, years ago—long time ago—I used to take care of her. Big brother, understand? When we was kids. She used to call me Chucky. Actually, Charley's my name. We grew up together."

"You did?"

"Right. Over by Park Slope. But I just wanted to find out that she's doing okay. Where do you live?"

"In the basement."

"Well, it's not easy to find rooms. Hey, sonny, wouldn't have an apple or something around, would you? Some bread?"

"Got lots of cold cereal."

"With milk?"

"Sure."

"That'll be something. You could bring it outside? Or, say—Chet you say your name was?—I could go around to the back. I mean, looking like this—not shaved, my clothes looking not too clean and all—people might call the cops. And I don't want any trouble. Oh, I'm telling you, sonny, I've had enough trouble."

"What kind of trouble?"

"Tell you what: you bring me some food, and I'll tell you all about it."

"HERE you are, mister."

"Hey, a whole box!"

"It's good-tasting golden rice flakes with loads and loads of valuable vitamins, minerals, and other vital food elements that help build strong, healthy bodies. It'll give you the pep and energy to be wide awake and husky. And you can have as much as you like. I just want the box top."

"What is that you just said, a poem?"

"Something I heard."

"Well, excuse my manners. I'll eat."

"Mister, can you tell me what kind of trouble you had?"

"Really want to know?"

"Yes."

"See, Chet, between you and me—I can trust you, can't I?"

"Yes, sir."

"Well, truth is, I just got out of prison."

"You did?"

"It's true."

"Were you a . . . public enemy?"

"Public enemy? What's that?"

"You know, a big-time crook."

"Big-time crook. . . . That's a good one. That what I look like? For me, little-time crook is more like it. That's what the law thought. Bookie, actually. Little-time bookie. That's what I was. You know what a bookie is?"

"No, sir."

"See, I worked the neighborhood for bets on horse races. Small-time stuff. Nickels and dimes. Not much of a living. Nothing big-time, you understand. Not for Chucky. Nope, I wasn't one of the big boys. But I got by. I did. Not bad hours either. See, my angle was I used to get all my dope on this sort of radio station I set up. A wire hookup."

"Oh, wow."

"Sure. At first the cops couldn't figure how I got the results so fast. But someone squealed. Chet, take it from me. Stay on that old straight and narrow. Doing what I did— What did you call it? Public enemy. Makes me laugh. Wasn't worth it. Believe me. Nine years in the slammer. . . . But I got parole when I promised to enlist in the army. What do you call this stuff?"

"Rogers' *POW!*"

"You don't say. I could use some *POW!*"

"There's a model soldier in the box. I've got three sets, so you can have it if you want."

"Naw. You keep it. Now look here, Chet. You have to promise me something. You have to promise not to say anything about my being here to my sister."

"Okay . . ."

"I was going to call her, but I found out she doesn't have a phone. And I didn't want to write. To tell the truth, I'm not so good at writing. But I had to make sure. Understand? My sister and all. It's been nine years. But you said she's doing okay. Well, that's a load off."

"I brought this apple too."

"You're a good kid. All right. Hey, you go to school?"

"Yeah. But it's boring."

"Boring? Try nine years in Sing Sing. Okay, I'll be off. Thanks for the food. And you ain't going to tell anyone, right? That a deal? Shake on it? Just you and me. You can call me Uncle Charley. What did you say your name was?"

"Chet Barker."

"Sounds like a movie star. That's okay. You and me. Nice talking to you, Chet. Public enemy. I like that. Remember, mum's the word."

"Good luck. . . ."

"Episode 15"

"ALL RIGHT, class. It's time to take out our readers again. We're going to start a whole new chapter today. It begins on page two hundred and ninety-five. It's called 'Bob Goes to the Dentist.' Who wants to start off reading? Franklin, is that really you?"

"Yes, Miss Gomez."

"Fine. I'm delighted. Have the place, everybody? You can start, Franklin."

"Okay. 'One sunny morning when Bob woke up, his mouth was hurting painfully. "Oh, mother," Bob said while at the breakfast table, "I think I had better go to the dentist." "Is something the matter?" she asked. "I think so," Bob replied. "Well, Bob," said his father, "have you been brushing your teeth after each and every meal the way you should if you want strong, white teeth and healthy gums?" "Oh, yes, sir, I have. You know I do." ' But last night after dinner I ate seven thousand gob stickers, a zillion Black Crows—"

"Class! Franklin!"

"What?"

"That's *not* what's in the book. Please read only what's there. A writer's words should always be *sacred*. They choose each one carefully."

"Well, if I were the writer, one of those gob stickers would have this magic mixture that turns him into a gigantic head louse—"

"Class! Sheli, I think you can read now."

"But—"

"Franklin, you know what I'm going to say, don't you?"

"You probably want me to stay after school."

"Exactly."

"Neat-o."

"THIS IS Thursday, Franklin. Did your parents receive my letter?"

"Yes, ma'am."

"What did they say?"

"They said they would be charmed to see you at the time you set forth."

"*Charmed?*"

"That's what they said."

"I doubt it. But whatever they said, I truly intend

to be there. And you might as well know I'm going to tell them I'm recommending that you be left back a year."

"I know."

"Don't you care?"

"I do. I do a lot."

"Franklin, I mean it. I'm going to be there at seven o'clock sharp."

"SKIPPER, it's working!"

"Miss Gomez really coming over?"

"She kept me in after school specially to tell me she would."

"You made her keep you in, didn't you?"

"Had to make sure."

"Think your parents will really be out when she comes?"

"Sure."

"Don't you think you better check?"

"My father's working. And my mother promised to go to the meeting. Skipper, it's time we headed out."

"Where to, Chet?"

"Pearlman's. We have to call her."

"Who?"

"Miss Gomez."

"Why?"

"Skipper, you know as well as I do you always have to give a final warning."

"HAND ME the nickel."

"You know, one of these days—"

"Shhh! It's ringing. Miss Gomez? This is your masked friend. Everything is—"

"What happened?"

"She hung up."

"Oh-oh."

"What?"

"You didn't give her a final warning."

"Skipper, it's a chance we'll have to take."

"MA?"

"What?"

"You're going to that meeting tonight, right?"

"What meeting?"

"Ma! I told you! At school."

"Maybe."

"Ma! You said you'd go. You did! And, Ma, I told Miss Gomez you would. All the other kids' parents are going. The class that gets a hundred percent attendance gets a prize!"

"I don't know. I'm awful tired."

"Ma, *please*. You have to. You can't be the only one not going. You really promised!"

"Tell me again what it's about."

"About what class I'll be in next year."

"Why do they have to have a meeting about that? Never had one before."

"I told you. This is different."

"Why?"

"It just is."

"That's not an answer."

"You want the truth?"

"Of course."

"They want to give me an award."

"A what?"

"An award."

"Franklin, what are you talking about?"

"See, Miss Gomez picked me for the Student-with-the-Most-Potential Award. And it's going to be on the radio. And you get a prize because you're my mother. Ten dollars a week for the rest of your life. Really."

"Frankie, you would exhaust a dead person."

"Ma, my whole future depends on it! The whole future of the free world!"

"What time is the meeting?"

"I told you! Seven."

"Well, if you've promised, I suppose I should. Now get off your knees."

"TOM?"

"What's that, Frankie?"

"How you doing?"

"Fine."

"Feeling okay?"

"Yeah, sure."

"Guess what? Ma's going to a meeting at school."

"Yeah, she told me."

"And Pop's working."

"Right."

"And I'm supposed to be in the basement and not allowed to come out."

"You are out."

"Yeah, but I'm not supposed to be. So I just want to ask you if—you know—when they're not here, what happens if someone comes to the door?"

"Nothing."

"Aren't you going to answer it?"

"Nope."

"How come?"

"It's not going to be for me."

"It . . . could be."

"Not a chance."

"Tom, are you going to stay in here forever?"

"What's that supposed to mean?"

"Mr. Swerdlow's gone. You could move back to your old room, you know."

"Frankie, I'm doing fine right here."

"Tom, how come you're acting like this?"

"What's that supposed to mean?"

"People should look ahead. Accept disappointments and pay attention to the future, or life will pass you by."

"Frankie, you are one big enormous pain."

"Well, you're the only hero in the whole world acting the way you do."

"Maybe you'd better start believing I wasn't any hero."

"You are!"

"You know something, Frankie? If you don't look out, one of these days I'm going to tell you what it was *really* like."

"Boy . . . wish you would."

"You think you'd like it, don't you?"

"Be neat."

"Think it's so great?"

"Everyone knows it was."

"Don't be a sap, Frankie."

"Tom, why do you have to be so different from everyone else?"

"Think I am?"

"Know so."

"Frankie, what makes you think you know so much?"

"Because I listen to real radio, not that sappy, dumb music you play all the time!"

"Okay, kid, you're asking for it. I'm going to tell you what it was like—but I don't intend to say it again. *Ever!* You hear me? Do you?"

"Yeah. . . ."

"Frankie, when we hit that beach, we were scared. More scared than anything. Sick scared. So scared people were pissing in their pants. Whimpering. Crying. 'Cause we could see what was coming. Just knew it would be bad, real bad. Noise was bursting from so many different directions you couldn't hear yourself think. All you knew was that you were scared. But we hit that beach because that's what we had to do. And guys were scrambling and crawling and running every which way so you couldn't see nothing. People yelling, trying to be brave, trying to do what we were told. But screaming. Trying to move. Trying to use our rifles. But, see, the Japanese were ready for us. Bullets like fistfuls of pebbles coming at us hand after hand after hand. Explosions all over the place. You couldn't think. And the next thing, blood and bodies all over. People screaming. But a different kind of screaming and crying, Frankie. A kind I hope you never hear. Then I got hit. Like someone taking a two-by-four and whacking at my leg. *Wham! Wham!* I got knocked down. People running over me. Stepping on me. I was sure I was dead. And I was crying for Ma, and Pop, even you, Frankie, damn it, wishing, praying to God I was home. Right here. Right where I am now. So let me tell you something: I'm *lucky* to be alive! Lucky to be here. You know how many buddies of mine got it? A lot. So that's what it's like to be a hero like me. It stinks. Because I don't want to be told about being no hero. Load of crap! Now get the hell out of here and don't you talk to me about heroes again. You understand? Never!"

"HEY, FRANKIE, what's the matter?"

"Nothing."

"You look sick."

"I'm all right."

"Sure?"

"Yeah."

"Think Miss Gomez will come?"

"I don't know. What time is it?"

"Close to seven."

"Mario . . ."

"What?"

"I . . . I hope she doesn't come."

"What did you say?"

"It's a mistake."

"What is?"

"Doing this."

"You all right, Frankie?"

"Yeah."

"Frankie, what's the matter? What happened?"

"Nothing."

"Something did."

"Remember that bum the other day?"

"Yeah. What about him?"

"It was my uncle Charley."

"It was?"

"Yeah. He's a crook."

"Oh, boy. . . ."

"And another thing, about Tom . . ."

"What about him?"

"I know what's the matter with him now."

"What?"

"He almost died. Really died. Like your father. And he was so scared. Really scared. You should have heard him talk. Scared me."

"Frankie . . ."

"What?"

"Can I tell you something?"

"Yeah. . . ."

"It's about my father."

"What about him?"

"Promise never to tell anyone."

"Promise."

"Swear on your mother's mother's mother?"

"On my mother's mother's mother."

"Okay. . . . Sometimes . . . sometimes I'm glad my father isn't coming back."

"What do you mean? How come?"

"See, he used to make my mother cry a lot."

"Oh. . . ."

"Yeah. . . ."

"Oh, man. . . . Mario, you know what I like best about the radio?"

"What?"

"It's just about the only thing that makes any real sense."

"Frankie . . ."

"What?"

"You okay?"

"I just wish . . ."

"Frankie!"

"What?"

"Miss Gomez just came around the corner. She's heading this way."

"Oh, no. . . ."

"Hello, Miss Gomez."

"Hello, Mario. Hello, Franklin. Well, Franklin, I'm sure your parents are expecting me."

"Miss Gomez . . ."

"Yes, Franklin."

"Miss Gomez, my parents aren't here."

"I beg your pardon?"

"My father's working. My mother . . . went out."

"Franklin, you told me they'd be here. I think you said they would be charmed to see me."

"I lied."

"Franklin, is this another one of your dodges?"

"No, Miss Gomez. I'm telling the truth."

"Ummm. . . ."

"Think I better go home. See you, Frankie. Bye, Miss Gomez."

"Good-bye, Mario. Now, Franklin, I warned you. I fully intend to talk to your parents. They're expecting me."

"But, Miss Gomez, I just told you. They're not here."

"The door's open."

"For me."

"I think I'd better see for myself."

"But—"

"Mrs. Wattleson! Mr. Wattleson! Is anybody home?"

"See. I told you."

"Franklin, I really don't understand this. You promised they would be here. You practically bragged that they would."

"It was all a plot."

"A what?"

"A story. I made it up."

"Franklin, you're making me very angry."

"I'm sorry."

"And nobody's home?"

"Just my brother."

"What's his name?"

"Tom."

"Is he the one recently discharged from the army?"

"Yeah."

"Well, fine. I'm perfectly willing to speak to him."

"Miss Gomez, you mustn't go in—"

"Mr. Tom Wattleson! Are you there? Franklin, where is he?"

"Miss Gomez—"

"Where is he?"

"In his room upstairs."

"Mr. Wattleson! Franklin's brother! May I speak to you, please!"

"Miss Gomez, please! He won't come down."

"And why not?"

"He just won't."

"That's not an answer."

"See, he's all upset and— Miss Gomez, please, he doesn't want to be bothered."

"Franklin, do you know how angry I am? I came here because I care about you and . . . Now I want you to go to your brother immediately and tell him I must see him for a moment!"

"But—"

"Just do as I ask!"

"TOM . . ."

"Frankie, I thought I told you to keep away."

"Tom, I'm sorry, but—"

"Keep out of here, will you!"

"Tom . . . there's a lady . . . It's my teacher. Miss Gomez. She's downstairs. She wants Ma, or Pop, or . . ."

"That's got nothing to do with me."

"She wants to see you."

"*Me?*"

"That's what she says. Tom . . ."

"Frankie, what are you crying about? What is going on?"

"Tom, see, it's this whole plot I made up. I'm sorry, Tom. Really, I am. I didn't know. I just wanted you to meet her, because . . . I didn't know . . ."

"Franklin! Mr. Wattleson! Are you up there?"

"Just what the hell did you do, Frankie?"

"See, Tom, I was trying to help you and her because her boyfriend—"

"Franklin! I'm coming up."

"Look here, kiddo. I don't want anything to do with this dame. Understand? Not her. No one. Nothing. I don't want to see anybody! So get the hell out of here and tell her not to come up."

"Tom, she's standing at the foot of the steps. I think she's coming up."

"Of all the—"

"Tom, there's another way out."

"What?"

"There's another way out of the house."

"What?"

"There's a board under your bed. You can get over to Mario's."

"What are you talking about?"

"See, Mario and I used to go back and forth. You could do it. . . . But your leg—"

"Mr. Wattleson! I really must speak to you briefly!"

"Nothing the matter with my leg."

"There isn't?"

"Where's the board?"

"I'll get it. You get the window open."

"It's open. Now what?"

"Here's the board. Mario! Hey, Mario! Open your window!"

"What you doing, Frankie? Did Miss Gomez leave? Did your brother—"

"Mario, shut up. Fix the board."

"What's going on?"

"Just do it! Set?"

"Yeah."

"See, Tom, you can get over."

"Franklin? Mr. Wattleson?"

"Okay, Frankie, out of the way. This kid your friend Mario?"

"Yeah. Mario, this is my brother, Tom."

"Oh."

"Mario, that thing set? I'm coming over."

"But my mother—"

"Franklin? Where are you hiding?"

"Tom, hurry! She's up the stairs. She's coming down the hall."

"Okay, kid. Steady it."

"Frankie, it's cracking!"

"Tom!"

"Franklin, are you in here?"

"Tom! Tom! Are you all right? Tom?"

"Stupid board! Frankie, why didn't you tell me it was cracked!"

"What is going on . . . ?"

"Miss Gomez, help! My brother, Tom, just fell out the window. He's barely holding on—"

"Fell? Out the window? What are you talking about? *What* is going on here?"

"Hurry! My brother fell out of the window! He's holding on to the sill!"

"Let me see. . . . Oh, my God! Who is that?"

"It's my brother, Miss Gomez! Tom, hold on! Mario! Call the police!"

"Frankie, for God's sake, reach down and grab me, will ya? I'm losing my grip."

"I'm trying, Tom! Miss Gomez! Help!"

"Franklin, put your hands around my waist. Tighter! Brace yourself! Tighter. I'm going to lean out. . . . Mr. Wattleson, I'm trying to grab you by your belt. I've got it. Now, pull, Frankie . . . pull!"

"I'm pulling!"

"Hold on, Mr. Wattleson! Hold on! Ease in. There!"

"Tom, you okay?"

"Mr. Wattleson, are you all right?"

"Yeah. I'm all right."

"I don't understand. How did you manage to fall out the window?"

"I . . ."

"It was an accident."

"I assume it was an accident, Franklin, but—"

"Hi, Ma."

"Franklin, I just was at your school and— What is going on here?"

"Mrs. Wattleson, I'd like to introduce myself. My name is Esmeralda Gomez. I'm—"

"Tom, what is going on? . . . Why are you sitting on the floor? Who is this woman? What is she doing here?"

"Frankie!"

"Mario, please, be quiet! Tom, will you answer me?"

"I fell out of the window."

"You *what*?"

"I fell out of the window, and this lady—"

"But you're laughing!"

"Frankie! Hey, Frankie!"

"Mario, for goodness' sake! What is it?"

"Mrs. Wattleson, Frankie said to call the police. So I called them and the fire department. They said they'll be right over, and I think I hear the sirens."

"I don't understand any of . . . I thought there was a meeting at—"

"Mrs. Wattleson, I'm Franklin's sixth grade teacher. I came over because I wanted to talk to you and your husband about Franklin, who—"

"Ma!"

"Frankie, I am trying to talk to—"

"Mrs. Wattleson! Hurry! There are firemen out front!"

"Tom, please stop laughing for a moment!"

"Oh, hi, Pop!"

"What in God's name is going on around here? I come around the corner, and there are cops and fire engines standing outside. . . . Who is this woman?"

"Frankie's sixth grade teacher."

"Mr. Wattleson, how do you do? My name is Esmeralda Gomez—"

"Look, Tom, I don't want you sneaking women—"

"Pop!"

"Don't bother me—"

"But Pop—"

"For God's sake, what is it, Frankie?"

"The cops just smashed in the front door, and the firemen are bringing up the hoses."

"Episode 16"

"CHET BARKER, Master Spy!"

"Da-dum, da-dum!"

"The makers of Oriental Oat Pies bring you another thrilling adventure of Chet Barker, Master Spy! Chet Barker, smart and full of potential, fearless and well prepared. Chet Barker, soaring out of dim history to right the wrongs of life. He fights for what's right on land!"

"On the sea!"

"And in the air! With his faithful and loyal sidekick, Skipper O'Malley, Chet Barker—restored to his own, rightful room—believes that justice is worth struggling for!"

"Da-dum."

"And now, for today's adventure, The Wedding Night Caper!"

"Frankie, I'm not so sure we should be doing this."

"Mario, when the adventure's done and after the commercial, there's *always* a piece at the end."

"I know, but putting that microphone under Tom and Miss Gomez's bed—"

"Mario, she's Mrs. Wattleson now."

"You still got left back."

"Well, everything else worked. Mr. Swerdlow out. Tom back in his own room. Him being happy again. The war over. Then him and Miss Gomez getting married."

"Took them six months."

"They wanted to be sure. Anyway, I got my own radio."

"I know. Still . . . listening to them this way doesn't seem right. Not when they just got married. If my mother—"

"Mario, we got a new board. You can get back to your room quick. You know what your trouble is, Skipper? You don't have faith."

"In what?"

"Radio. What time is it?"

" 'Bout eleven."

"They should be there. . . ."

"Frankie . . . what if they find the microphone?"

"They won't."

"And they might just want to be—you know— private."

"We'll only listen for a few minutes. . . . Ready?"

"Suppose."

"Okay, Skipper, turn the Atomic Remote Relay Radio speaker on!"

"TOM, I'm really happy. I am."

"Me too."

"But you know . . . there's one thing I never told you."

"Oh?"

"It's sort of strange. . . ."

"You don't have to tell me."

"I know. . . . But, well, it wasn't long after I learned about Mitch being killed."

"Honey . . ."

"No, I want you to hear this. You know how . . . awful it was—and how I felt. Well, one day I was sitting in a park. Penny Bridge Park. I was crying. Just so miserable. I wasn't seeing anything. Then, all of a sudden—when I looked up—there, right in front of me—I couldn't believe it. A little person. Maybe a child. Or an elf. With a long coat down to his toes. And a hat on. A man's hat. And he was masked."

"Masked?"

"It was so extraordinary I could hardly believe what I was seeing, and then, it—in this squeaky voice—he said, 'Don't worry. I'll look out for you. Everything will be okay.' Then he began to *spell* something."

"You kidding?"

"And the next moment—he was gone. Ran away."

"Honey, you must have imagined it."

"I've often thought I did. But every now and again that moment comes back into my mind. The thing is, it must have been real. And it must have been a kid. But then, I keep asking myself, Who was that masked kid, anyway?"

"OH, MAN, Frankie, you did it!"

"Shucks, Skipper. 'Tweren't nothing. Nothing at all."